HER CLIENT
HIS MATCH

TAMICKA LEONARD

Hill Leonard PLLC
Texas

Published by Hill Leonard PLLC
ISBN: 979-8-9989269-9-0

Printed in the United States of America

www.tamickaleonard.com

tamickaleonard@gmail.com

First Edition

For my family

PART I

ROOMS OF GLASS

PROLOGUE

Noelle

In this city, names open doors. Mine opens something even more powerful—hearts. Collins & Co. isn't just a matchmaking firm—it's an institution whispered about at galas and etched into the gloss of society pages. My name moves through circles that pretend not to need me, families who trade discretion like currency. I built it match by match until Collins became more than a name—it became a brand of trust, desire, and quiet power.

My clients have everything: estates with gates taller than their secrets, portfolios thick enough to bow tables, legacies built on generations of control. And yet, they come to me for what their money can't command—love that feels unshakable. From Houston to New York to Los Angeles, I build relationships that look effortless, pairing influence with intimacy, strategy with chemistry until two people believe they've found forever.

I studied psychology, but life gave me a doctorate in human nature. I've learned to hear the truths tucked between sentences, to recognize longing behind practiced smiles, to see what someone needs long before they're ready to admit it. I know the difference between attraction that burns out and devotion that holds steady. To the outside world, I'm an alchemist turning chance into certainty. Behind closed doors, I am the architect of lives that appear seamless.

Yet despite all of that, being alone has become the backdrop of my life, even in the brightest rooms. I've celebrated love in ballrooms lit by chandeliers, signed contracts worth more than houses, orchestrated unions polished enough to silence gossip—and still, when the music fades and the papers are filed, I return home to silence. I thought I had found forever once, but it was smoke dressed as fire, promises written in disappearing ink. I survived it, and I never forgot.

What it did teach me—what I still believe—is that love isn't curated photographs or grand gestures designed for applause. It is the quiet rituals that repeat until they become marrow. My parents taught me that. Thirty-three years, and I watched them practice devotion in ways so ordinary they became extraordinary. My father replacing what broke before my mother could ask. My mother serving him the meals that brought him comfort even on her hardest days. And when cancer came, they held the line together, scarred but unbroken, walking side by side until the sickness retreated. Their love was flawed, sometimes tired, but it was constant.

That is what I carry into every match. Not perfection. Steadiness. Loyalty. The kind of love that chooses again and again, especially when the world tilts and nothing feels certain. That is the foundation I give to my clients.

And in all these years, I have not failed once.

Each morning, I stop on the sidewalk and lift my gaze to the silver letters gleaming against glass and steel.

Collins & Co.

My name. My work. My empire.

People see the sleek office, the tailored suits, the polished calm. They don't see the years before—the rented closet above a dry cleaner, the networking rooms where I walked in invisible and left exhausted but determined. They don't see the one person who believed in me when belief was all I had.

They doubted me. They still do. But I've learned doubt can be a motivator—and power is best built quietly.

So when they say I'm too young, too ambitious, too much, I just look up at those letters and think: you have no idea.

Then I square my shoulders, step through the revolving doors, and become who they expect to see—composed, unshakable, the woman who never misses.

On my desk, an espresso waits—dark, rich—beside a leather file stamped confidential.

Inside: a man who doesn't believe in love. A man who treats hearts like mergers and vows like liabilities. The one client everyone warned me not to take.

They say he can't be matched.

I say they've never met me.

CHAPTER 1
Silk Over Glass

Noelle

Sadie, my assistant, knocked once before stepping in, her sleek bob swaying as she leaned against the walnut frame.

"Your next appointment is here," she said with her usual crisp efficiency. "Valeria Alvarez."

I slid the file into my desk and tapped the corner of my iPad, pulling up her profile.

"Thank you, Sadie. Send her in."

Heels back on, spine straightened into the posture drilled into me since childhood. My grandmother always said: *When you're about to meet someone's heart, you'd better look like you take it seriously.* I made sure I did, every time.

Valeria swept in on a faint cloud of Baccarat Rouge, her heels clicking against the marble inlay. Confidence radiated from her—cream blazer, silk blouse, flawless blowout—but her eyes betrayed her nerves. I could already tell she was a woman used to controlling her million dollar business with ease, but not her own heart.

She slid into the chair, diamond bracelet catching the light.

"It's nice to meet you, Valeria," I said warmly, rising from behind my glass desk. "I've reviewed your profile, but this is our time to go deeper. Tell me—in your own words—what are you hoping for?"

"Well, he has to be tall—six foot two, minimum. He needs to earn more than I do, but also have the flexibility to drop everything if I want to fly to Paris on a Tuesday. Handsome, obviously. Educated, Ivy League preferred. No kids, and preferably no ex-wives. Too much baggage. Adventurous, but not reckless—he should know how to sail a yacht and protect me. Loves to travel, but only first class or private. Grounded, but not boring. And—" she leaned forward, dead serious—"he cannot snore. Not even lightly. If he does, it's over."

One brow arched. "Noted. No snoring. Anything else? Should I make sure he whips up Michelin-star meals, doubles as your personal trainer, and serenades you over morning coffee?"

Her eyes lit with excitement. "Wait—really?"

A laugh threatened to burst out, but I smothered it with nothing more than a look.

She caught herself, then laughed outright. Her posture eased. "Oh—you were joking. My apologies. I suppose I did get a little ahead of myself there…"

The corner of my mouth lifted. "It's my job to bring you back." I set my tablet aside.

"Here's the truth. Lists are common. Everyone has them. But lists don't keep you warm when the flight's canceled in Barcelona. Lists don't make you laugh after a miserable day. Lists don't pull you back when you start to lose yourself."

Valeria's smile faltered—softened.

I leaned in, my voice steady, threaded with quiet insistence. "So let me ask you this instead. Forget the galas. Forget the family Christmas card. When you picture partnership—the moments no one else sees—what do you see?"

Her façade cracked. Eyes dropped, fingers tightening against the armrest. "I see… Sunday mornings. Cooking breakfast together. Bike rides. Someone who wants to talk about everything and nothing and whose presence is comforting after a long day. Someone who looks at me and sees *Valeria*—not Valeria Alvarez from the Alvarez family. My last name turns every date into a business pitch."

That admission landed heavy. I felt it—the weight of years where power eclipsed tenderness, where her brilliance had been treated like something to negotiate instead of a gift.

I softened, but let conviction edge my voice. "That's it. That's the vision we build toward. Not a résumé or a list. Just the rhythm of your real life—with the right person beside you."

Her voice dropped, raw. "I need someone who will *actually pursue me*. A lot of wealthy men think effort is optional because women are already lined up. I'm not starved for a man—but for the one who will choose me and fight for me, even when he knows he already has me."

Her words struck deep. I knew that ache—the longing not just to be chosen, but to be cherished.

"You deserve more than a man who treats you like an option," I told her, leaning in so she could feel the certainty in my voice. "The right one won't sit back. He'll show you—over and over—that you matter. That you're worth the effort."

Her exhale broke loose, shoulders easing as if she'd finally set down a burden no one else had noticed. "I actually feel… lighter saying all this out loud."

I smiled, warm, certain. "That's because you finally named it. You don't want to chase—you want to be earned. And you should expect nothing less."

She left with a stride carrying more hopefulness than when she arrived.

Back at my desk, my pen tapping once against the folder, I wrote in black ink:

Don't just find her a match. Find her an equal.

Sadie poked her head back in just as I finished my notes on Valeria.

"Your next appointment should be here any minute," she said softly.

I slid Valeria's file aside and pulled the thick leather folder out of the drawer. The calfskin gave off a faint, expensive scent as I flipped it open, eyes narrowing at the name stamped across the top.

"Ezra Sinclair," I murmured, letting the syllables roll off my tongue like top-shelf bourbon. The dossier was stacked with receipts of power: generational wealth multiplied into empires. Real estate. Tech. Luxury brands. A man who didn't gamble unless the outcome was already fixed. Untouchable. I was more than familiar with his type.

My pen tapped against the page, a smile tugging at my mouth.

"Let's see if you're as formidable as they say."

Minutes dragged. Twenty. Thirty. Forty-five. Each tick of the Cartier clock stitched irritation tighter in my chest. By the time forty-five minutes passed, My patience was gone.

Sadie reappeared, tablet in hand. "Still nothing. Want me to call his office?"

I didn't look up. "No. Calling him would only feed his ego. If this is how he intends to conduct himself, I have no problem canceling his contract. Can't pay me enough to endure disrespect. I'm an expert, not his employee."

The folder shut with a decisive snap. Legs crossed, posture coiled into deliberate composure. He thought lateness conferred power. Perhaps it did in his world. But if Ezra Sinclair believed wealth freely entitled him to my time, he was sadly mistaken.

Movement in the hall. Sadie's startled voice cut through: "Excuse me—you can't just walk in here like that!"

The door swung open.

Ezra Sinclair entered as though the air bent around him. Charcoal wool poured seamless over broad shoulders, tapering to a lean waist. His build said he spent hours in the mornings at the gym. He stood tall enough that the gilded molding above my door nearly brushed his head.

A muted curl of Tom Ford Oud Wood followed him, threading through the office until it settled in my lungs. He adjusted a cufflink with unhurried arrogance—no rush, no apology. A man for whom denial appeared to be an unfamiliar language.

Eyes—dark brown, unreadable—swept the room until they landed on me, cool and assessing.

Mahogany skin that caught the light, flawless in a way that made you want to find a line or wrinkle just to prove he was human. Full lips tipping into the faintest smirk. The audacity of a man amused by the very patience he'd wasted. It scraped against my nerves, daring me to cross the room and really put him in his place.

For a second, I registered the heat of him, the sheer weight of his presence. Magnetic. Infuriating. Exactly the kind of pull I refused to acknowledge.

I didn't rise. I let the silence sharpen between us like a blade.

Finally, after sighing like I was bored and already over him, I spoke, my voice silk over glass.

"Mr. Sinclair. How very generous of you… to keep me waiting for forty-five minutes."

CHAPTER 2

Terms and Conditions

Ezra

"Mr. Sinclair. How very generous of you… to keep me waiting for forty-five minutes."

Her tone wasn't sharp—it was surgical.

"Then I hope you used the time well," I said, crossing the room.

"I did. I learned how long it takes you to stretch my patience thin."

Her eyes lifted slowly, calm and unimpressed. Most people scrambled when I entered a room—voices quickening, gestures tightening, eyes darting to gauge what pleased me. She didn't.

She looked at me once, irritation slipping through her composure, and dismissed me with the kind of restraint that was more cutting than open defiance. It was the look of someone who had already measured me, filed me under predictable, and decided I wasn't worth the time I'd cost her.

That made her more interesting than the ones who fumbled.

I shut the door with a quiet click that landed heavier than any slam. For a moment, I couldn't move. The authority I carried into every room hesitated at the threshold. It was me who felt measured, the balance of power shifting before I could stop it.

Then she spoke.

"I imagine punctuality is optional when you think you own the clock."

The words were soft, but they struck like stone.

She sat there with her back straight, the faintest edge sharpening her eyes, and somehow that gaze pressed against my collar heavier than I expected. I should've brushed it off, the way I did with others. Instead, I absorbed it, irritation coiling in my chest at the fact that she'd gotten under my skin at all. This shouldn't have been difficult—match the right families, the right circles, the right pedigree. I could have handled it myself if I had the time. But time was the one currency I refused to waste, and so I was here, conceding the task to a stranger.

My plan was simple: dismiss her quickly, efficiently, without letting her linger.

And yet… something about her anchored me in place.

It wasn't the black blazer or the silk blouse—elegant, yes, but unremarkable. What caught me was the woman inside them. Spirals of hair framed her face with deliberate grace, each curl pulling the eye toward high cheekbones and lips pressed into composure sharp enough to cut. Warm, caramel-toned skin glowed under the filtered light of the office. Her body carried the clothes, not the other way around, posture radiating a quiet authority that belonged to her alone.

She didn't need to command attention. She simply had it. A beauty that worked like gravity. Subtle. Constant. Impossible to resist once you stepped into its orbit. And worse, she made no effort to hide her displeasure.

I tilted my head, voice flat, testing her. "Word is you're the best. Convince me this isn't a waste of my time."

She smirked, subtle and sure. "Mr. Sinclair, I don't convince. I deliver."

Not arrogance. Conviction.

Most women in my orbit turned themselves into performances—laughter rehearsed, glances calculated, gestures engineered for effect. Noelle Collins didn't. She carried herself like someone who already belonged, audience or not. And that unsettled me more than I cared to admit.

"Tell me what it is you're truly seeking."

I leaned against the chair across from her desk, deliberately not sitting, unwilling to concede that much ground. "The file says enough. Everything you need is there."

Her brow lifted, the motion small but edged. "Files tell me who you want the world to see. But what I read between the lines—that's where the truth lives."

I met her gaze, unblinking. "Files do matter. Background. Education. Family. Assets. Facts you can measure. Chemistry fades. Feelings change. Credentials last. All I need is someone whose background matches mine—and has a tolerable personality."

Her eyes sharpened. Not with offense. With curiosity.

"So you've convinced yourself love doesn't exist."

"Love," I said evenly, "is a story designed to distract people from the terms they're really living under."

She leaned forward, her voice quiet but edged like glass.

"You can hire staff from a résumé, Mr. Sinclair. But a life partner isn't an employee you can terminate. This is someone standing beside you when life turns unstable, unpredictable, human. A résumé won't hold you together when everything else falls apart."

Her gaze didn't waver. Brown eyes flecked with hazel held mine with unnerving steadiness. Her lashes swept low, then lifted again, deliberate—like she was stripping back layers I hadn't agreed to show.

The silence between us stretched, taut enough to make my composure itch. I forced air into my lungs, reminding myself why I was here.

Finally, I gave her something real, if only to end the stalemate. "What I avoid is neediness. Women who are draining. I don't want chaos mistaken for passion. I don't want someone who folds under pressure, or whose loyalty I'd have to question. At my level, marriage isn't about butterflies. It's about alignment. A partnership. Everything else is fantasy."

Her expression didn't change, but something shifted. Not judgment. Softer. Almost compassion. And that cut sharper than anything else because I knew it wasn't calculated.

She'd already read past the words, past the curtains I kept drawn.

"You keep people at a distance because it feels safe," she said softly. "But safe isn't strong. Safe is just another word for alone."

The strike was too deep.

For a moment, I wanted to shut her down—remind her exactly who she was speaking to. But I didn't. Because she wasn't guessing. She was certain.

Heat climbed under my skin, sharp and unwelcome.

"This is pointless, Ms. Collins," I said, tone clipped. "We're finished here."

She didn't react. She simply slid her pen back into her hand with surgical calm.

"If you could handle it yourself, Mr. Sinclair," she said evenly, "you wouldn't have walked through my door."

I left, outwardly composed, but her words followed, sharper than they had any right to be—the echo of her voice, the certainty in her eyes, the truth I hadn't asked for and couldn't seem to shake.

The car waited at the curb. I slid inside, jaw set, silence settling heavy as lead. The door shut, muting the city until only the hum of the engine and the thud of my own pulse remained.

The leather seat creaked as I shifted, my gaze catching on the gold crest embossed into the portfolio beside me. *Sinclair Holdings.* My grandfather built it brick by brick. My father turned it into an empire. Now it sits in my hands—both inheritance and weapon. Every deal, every acquisition, every sleepless night I bled into it wasn't out of obligation. I wanted this. The company is mine. It always will be.

What I don't want is the theater around it.

That's what this was—sitting in an office with a stranger I wouldn't have hired, listening to things I hadn't asked to hear. All I needed was for her to do her job so I could protect mine.

It had been my mother's suggestion. Not an order—strategy. *If anyone can manage this in six months, it's Noelle Collins. She understands our world. She'll know what's required.* Delivered the way she delivered everything: matter-of-fact, stripped of sentiment, weighted with calculation.

Quite honestly, she'd earned the right to be listened to. She steadied my father through decades of market swings, carried Sinclair Holdings' reputation on her shoulders when the numbers bled red, and kept the board aligned when their patience frayed. When she spoke, people listened. So did I—even when it cut against what I wanted.

If it were up to me, I wouldn't be marrying at all. Not now. Maybe not ever. But the board wanted stability. A fiancée gave them that. A wife sealed the deal. I could fight them on timing, on conditions—but not necessity.

That gnawed at me as I sat across from Noelle Collins. She met me head-on. That certainty. Her refusal to back down. That kind of resolve was rare. Dangerous. And I hated that it affected me—but that didn't mean I believed her illusions. Love wasn't real. It wasn't dependable. It was a distraction.

The irritation coiled until I cut it short with a flick of my thumb, pulling out my phone.

"Mother."

Her voice slid through the line, smooth as steel. "How did it go?"

"It didn't," I said flatly. "This isn't worth my time."

A pause. Measured. Then her tone shifted—low, absolute. "Ezra, you know what's at stake."

"I don't give a—"

"Yes, you do." Calm. Certain. "You've worked too hard for Sinclair Holdings to let the board doubt you now. Six months. No engagement, no seat. They won't wait."

Her words left no openings. My mother never argued. She closed doors until only one remained.

"This family's legacy has always been larger than any one man. Protect the legacy, Ezra. Protect your claim to it. Noelle Collins is your best chance. Don't waste it."

The line went dead. Verdict delivered. Agreement assumed.

I sat back, fingers drumming against the armrest, the question circling, heavier than it should have been. Was any of this worth it? The scrutiny. The intrusion. The weight of being measured by her.

I hated being maneuvered. But pride doesn't protect legacies. Pride doesn't bend boardrooms.

So I would go back. Not because I trusted her process, or anything she was trying to convince me of.

I would go back because survival demanded it.

And I refused to lose.

CHAPTER 3

Terms of Engagement

Noelle

The door shut with a quiet finality, but Ezra Sinclair's presence lingered like static after lightning. The air still vibrated with him—sharp, charged, impossible to ignore.

I sat motionless, pen balanced between my fingers, but the weight of him pressed into the room. His voice, low and unhurried, still reverberated in my chest. That sound belonged to men who expected the world to rearrange around them— baritone edged with command, the kind that didn't have to rise to be heard.

And his scent—smoke mixed with something warm and wood-rich—clung to the leather chairs, to the silk of my blouse, to me. I hated that I noticed. Hated more that my body catalogued it before my mind could intervene.

I exhaled, slow and deliberate. Maybe I'd cut too close. My words had slid beneath his armor faster than I intended, and the flicker in his eyes told me he'd felt it. But what was I supposed to do? Coddle him? Pretend I didn't see the truth of a man who built fortresses and called it freedom?

That wasn't my work. My work was clarity—and clarity didn't flinch.

I turned back to his file, ready to write the note still forming in my mind, when the door opened again.

Ezra Sinclair filled the doorway as though he hadn't left at all. His suit caught the light, dark wool cut to a body that radiated discipline. He didn't simply enter the room—he occupied it, shoulders squared, gaze steady, jaw locked in a line of authority. His movements were intentional, economical, and more unnerving because of it.

He checked his Patek with a flick of his wrist before sliding into the chair, the gesture less about the time and more about reminding me whose clock he believed we were on. Then, without waiting for an invitation, he lowered himself into the chair opposite me, the leather creaking as though conceding its place.

"Let's resume," he said. The words were even, but his voice slid across the desk—smooth as bourbon, heat curling beneath restraint.

I closed the folder. Set my pen aside. Met his gaze. "You were almost an hour late, Mr. Sinclair. And you've already walked out once. I don't restart what someone else ends."

For a moment, disbelief cracked his composure. His brows pulled together, reaction sharp, unguarded. It was gone in seconds, smoothed away beneath practiced control—but I saw it. The flicker of a man unused to resistance.

"Seriously?" The word slipped out low, half incredulous, more to himself than to me.

I rose, slow and steady, crossing to the door. Opened it. "Speak with my receptionist if you'd like to reschedule."

He didn't move. Not at first. The refusal was in the stillness, in the way he sat a beat too long, body tense as though absorbing the insult. Ezra Sinclair was clearly not a man who was used to being dismissed.

Then, finally, he stood. Void of urgency. Jacket buttoning with a flick of his fingers. The controlled movements of a man used to dictating the terms, even in retreat.

When he stepped closer, the air shifted with him, a subtle pressure that tightened around my lungs. At the threshold, he stopped. Looked down at me. His eyes, dark and unyielding, lingered too long, assessing—peeling me back layer by layer.

Beneath the steel, something flickered. Something I refused to name.

My pulse betrayed me anyway—skipped once, hard enough that I forced my breath to steady before it could give me away.

His mouth curved, faint and humorless, as though he'd just run into a problem he wasn't accustomed to solving in the moment.

Then he left.

I shut the door behind him, palm flat against the wood. My heartbeat was quick, insistent, an unruly rhythm I refused to acknowledge aloud.

He had walked out first.

And this time, I had shown him the door.

As soon as he was gone, I stacked the files with crisp precision, reclaiming control from the disruption his presence carried.

Ezra Sinclair was exactly what my sources warned me he'd be: brilliant, disciplined, immovable. A man who believed he'd already cracked the system, that marriage was nothing more than a contract. Men like him didn't come to me because they believed in love. They came because family or circumstance forced their hand.

I'd seen it before. But never with quite this much resistance.

It was going to be difficult—maybe the most difficult match I'd ever taken on. But impossible? No. Nothing was too impossible for me.

I drew a line beneath his name and wrote in the margin, in a firm, precise hand: *Requires strategy. Do not let him dictate the pace.*

Then I closed the file, slid it back into the drawer, and rose from my chair. Whatever Ezra Sinclair thought of me, whatever disbelief lingered in his eyes as he walked out, one fact remained: he knew he needed me and came back, however reluctantly.

That was all I needed.

Mr. Sinclair would fight me every step of the way, but that only sharpened my resolve.

He wasn't my first challenge. And he wouldn't be the one to break my record.

Brennan's had a way of making even a Tuesday night feel like an event. White tablecloths gleamed under soft light, silver chimed faintly against porcelain, and waiters in pressed jackets glided with the precision of a ballet. Butter, spice, blackened fish, and warm bread scented the air. Outside, Houston stretched restless and humid, horns and neon flashing a thousand promises. Inside, it felt like a symphony— orchestrated to make you forget the world pressing at the door.

Shayla was already waiting when I walked in, curls catching the chandelier's glow. Her expression was warm but edged with curiosity, like she'd been reading my mood before I even reached the table. That was Shayla—closest thing I had to a sister. She knew my truths without me needing to say them. Around her, there was no performance, no strategic charm, no worrying about how a word might land. With her, I could finally exhale after holding my breath all day.

She rose half out of her seat and hugged me, a quick, grounding squeeze. "About time," she teased, lifting her wine. "I was starting to think one of your hopeless romantics had stolen you away."

"Please." I set my clutch down, smoothing my skirt as I sat. "You're the only one who can drag me out after a day like this."

"Mm-hm." She tilted her glass, grin widening. "Meanwhile, my husband is at home destroying the couch cushions, yelling at ESPN like they can hear him. Just so you know, every time I'm dragged across the country to the Super Bowl—plus any other game he wants to see—I blame you."

I broke a piece of bread, laughing. "You're welcome?"

She pointed her fork at me, mock-accusing. "Don't play dumb. You're the one who shoved me toward him in college and told me to quit wasting time on boys who thought ramen counted as fine dining. Now look—married, happy, occasionally annoyed. All your fault."

"And yet every time he drives across town to bring you soup if you so much as sneeze, you forget to blame me," I countered.

Her expression softened, warmth slipping through. "That part, I'll thank you for forever."

The ease of friendship stretched between us, a familiar warmth layered with years of shared jokes and rescues, before she tipped her head, eyes narrowing playfully. "All right. Enough about me. What's going on with you? And don't give me the cookie-cutter version. I want the raw truth."

I exhaled, leaning back. "Honestly? It's a new client. I've only met him once—once—and I already know he's going to drive me insane."

Her brows shot up, delighted. "Ooooh, this I need to hear."

"It's not what you think," I warned, reaching for my glass. "He's arrogant. Shows up almost an hour late like I couldn't possibly have anything else to do. Walks in without apology, moves through the room like he owns it, and reduces my work to matching résumés. That part didn't surprise me; men like him rarely understand what matchmaking requires— at least not the way I do it."

"Then why are you still wound up?"

I swirled my wine, hesitating. "Because it's the way he does it. Like he's above the rules. Like the work I do isn't important…" My voice trailed.

Shayla's eyes gleamed. "And?"

I sighed. "He's the kind of man who thinks he can get away with anything because women usually let him. It doesn't help that he's tall, athletic, and smells maddeningly good. The whole package. He knows it. He uses it. But newsflash—it doesn't work on me."

Shayla nearly choked on her drink, laughing. "Handsome, eh? Now we're getting somewhere."

I groaned. "That is not the point. I've been there, done that—remember?"

She shot me the sideways look I knew too well. "Let's not waste time on *him*. I'm still stuck on the great Noelle Collins being rattled after one meeting. You brushed off that oil tycoon who tried to enroll his mistress without even blinking. But this guy? He's already under your skin?"

I pressed a hand to my temple. "Don't remind me of the mistress story."

Her grin widened, wicked. "Exactly. Not even that fiasco had you like this. This is different, and you can't convince me otherwise."

I straightened my napkin, refusing to rise to it. "He's a client, Shayla. That's all. I'm not letting him mess with my peace—or downplay what I do."

She lifted both hands in mock surrender, though her smile was too knowing. "Fine, I'll let it rest. For now. But I've known you since freshman year of high school, Noelle. If one meeting has you this worked up, I don't care how you frame it—you like whatever this is."

I shook my head, smirking despite myself. "You read too much into things."

"Mm-hm," she said, sipping her wine like a verdict. "We'll see."

I let the quiet settle, then gave her the part I'd been holding. "My work is important to me. I broke my "don't date a client" rule once and I regret that decision. I won't be doing it again."

Her hand found mine, warm and steady. "I understand where you're coming from. Just know the right man won't ask you to compromise your dreams. He'll make room—and stand in it with you."

Her words lingered—gentle, heavy enough to stay. That was Shayla: my anchor, my mirror, my sister in everything but blood. And whether I admitted it or not, she wasn't entirely wrong.

CHAPTER 4

Queens on the Board

Noelle

Sadie's laptop blinked open; she sat ramrod-straight, fingers poised over the trackpad. She made lists that solved problems before I'd finished naming them. I trusted her because she made messy days behave. She wasn't just my assistant anymore; she was my second set of eyes, my strategist, the ballast when the work stacked too high.

"I've narrowed Weston's shortlist to three," she said, nudging the laptop so I could see. "Profiles line up, compatibility scores are solid. If we move now, I can schedule first introductions by Friday."

"Perfect." I made a quick note in Weston's file. "Start with the Dallas heiress. She has the stability he needs without the drama."

"Done." Her fingers flew, then stilled. She tipped her head, study in her gaze that had nothing to do with Weston. "Do you want to keep talking about him—or circle back to the client who had you pacing yesterday?"

My pen paused mid-stroke. "No, thanks."

"I've sat at this desk since the day you hung the sign. I've watched you handle CEOs, senators, and men with more ego than assets. Not one of them made you this…

I said evenly. "I am just trying to do my job."

Sadie leaned closer, eyes twinkling with humor. "This job usually doesn't arrive with flushed cheeks."

I slid her a look over my glasses. "Sadie."

She leaned back, arms folded, grin tugging. "Okay, but can we at least acknowledge he's fine? Because, Noelle—whew. Let's be honest."

"You're confusing arrogance with attraction."

She laughed. "Please. Arrogance has never stopped half this city from drooling. Man walks in like he owns the oxygen—people inhale on command."

"Not me." I smoothed the edge of Ezra's file. "Clients are clients. He's no different."

"If you say so." She tapped the keyboard, eyes still dancing. "So… too late for me to add myself to his match queue?"

"Sadie." The warning lived in my tone.

She lifted both hands, surrendering, even as mischief shone. "Fine. He's just a client. A ridiculously attractive, very wealthy client with a stare that makes you tingle, but—just a client."

I squared a stack of papers with ordered calm. "Exactly."

Her laugh lingered, then she pivoted back to work.

The intercom hummed. "Ms. Collins, Mrs. Evelyn Sinclair is here to see you. Shall I send her in?"

Sadie's brows shot up before she schooled them smooth. She didn't need to say a word; her glance said everything about surprise visits at this level. She rose and slipped out.

I closed Ezra's file with a clean snap, "Send her in."

***

I stood instinctively, smoothing my blazer. Moments later, Evelyn Sinclair entered with the kind of poise that belonged less to a woman than to an institution. Tall, slender, every line of her navy silk dress cut to perfection. Pearls glowed at her throat, a diamond watch catching the light at her wrist, and her hair, swept into a smooth chignon, revealed a face that wore elegance the way others wore armor.

"Ms. Collins," she said warmly, extending her hand. "At last."

Her voice carried a musical cadence—measured, without heaviness. When I took her hand, her grip was cool and firm, the kind of practiced touch that conveyed pleasant authority.

"Mrs. Sinclair. What an honor."

She smiled—wide enough to feel genuine, restrained enough to remind me she never gave more than she intended.

Sliding into the chair opposite my desk, she crossed her legs in one fluid motion.

"I've heard remarkable things about you," she said, tone smooth as aged wine. "How you don't just pair people—you recalibrate them."

Her words weren't flattery. They were a test—like a chess player eyeing a piece before moving it.

"I do try," I replied carefully. "People come to me because they want to be seen, not just matched."

Her eyes softened. "Exactly. And Ezra…" She trailed off, lips curving as though the very name carried weight. "Ezra needs someone who can see him for who he is—and for who he refuses to admit he could be. You're not intimidated by him. That matters."

Warmth bloomed in my chest, unbidden. Coming from Evelyn Sinclair, this wasn't just approval—it felt like an anointment.

"I appreciate you saying that," I said sincerely.

She inclined her head, pearls at her ears catching the light. "Of course, I only want what's best for my son. But I've also spent my life protecting an empire with his name on it. That means I look at him both as a mother and as a board chair. Ezra is brilliant, but brilliance unchecked can become volatility. He needs someone who balances him, steadies him, and understands that partnership is not sentiment—it's strategy."

It appeared that for her, maternal pride and corporate oversight blurred until they were indistinguishable.

Her smile didn't falter, but the steel beneath it was unmistakable. "We've invested considerably in this process, Ms. Collins. A financial package of this size isn't charity. It's a contract. And contracts demand results."

Her words soothed; the meaning did not. A reminder that even love, in her world, could be reduced to terms and deliverables.

"I understand," I said evenly, posture unyielding. "You'll see results."

"I expect nothing less," she replied. Then, softer, but no less precise: "Still, there are women I know—women of refinement, discretion, legacy. Names that would strengthen Ezra in the eyes of our world. If you'd like, I can pass a few along."

The suggestion was delivered lightly, as though offering a courtesy. But the precision made it clear: she was floating her own candidates, sanctioned and approved.

I smiled as though unruffled. "Thank you. I'll review them."

For the first time, her gaze drifted to the desk, where Ezra's file lay half-open. Her fingers brushed the strap of her Birkin. Her eyes lingered on the name embossed across the folder—just a moment too long.

Then she looked back, her smile intact. "I have faith in you, Ms. Collins. Truly."

When she rose, she did so with the same quiet command she'd carried in, leaving behind the faint trace of a French perfume threaded with oakmoss—and the ripple of approval I hadn't realized I wanted until I had it.

The door closed gently behind her.

I stood in the hush she'd left behind, oddly buoyed. Evelyn Sinclair was on my side. Ezra might be a storm—but storms could be steered.

Still, her smile nagged at me—too practiced, too sharp. Like a queen already three moves ahead on a board I wasn't aware I was on.

***

Evelyn

The door shut softly behind me, sealing me in the leather quiet of the town car. The driver pulled forward, tires humming against the pavement, but my eyes stayed fixed on the folder across my lap. Ezra's name, stamped in bold across the front.

My oldest son. My greatest prize.

Of all the things I've built, defended, sacrificed for—Ezra is the proof it wasn't in vain. Brilliant, disciplined, relentless. He took Sinclair Holdings further than Robert ever dared, expanded into markets seasoned men tiptoed around. He is everything his grandfather would have expected of him, and more.

And still—it isn't enough.

Not for the board. Not for the men who hover like vultures, sniffing for weakness. Thirty-five. Unmarried. To them, those aren't personal choices. They're liabilities. Every Sinclair man before Ezra was married by now. Every one of them secured an alliance that shored up the company's image and safeguarded the empire. Ezra's bachelorhood? They call it "optics." What they mean is cracks.

And I know how quickly cracks become weapons.

When Charles died, Robert was barely in his thirties. Brilliant but untested. His uncle wasted no time circling— whispering to the directors that Robert wasn't ready, that Sinclair Holdings needed a man of experience. It was the closest the company ever came to slipping away. Robert fought in the boardroom, but I fought everywhere else—quiet dinners, phone calls, steady reminders of where loyalty belonged. By the time the board convened, the coup was already dead.

The memory never left me. Neither did the fear.

And now it's Ezra's turn. Ezra, who has earned every inch of his place, who bleeds for this company. And yet, they question him. Too young. Too unsteady. Too alone. The same poison, recycled.

I love all of my children—deeply, differently—but Ezra is the one the legacy rests on. Julian is brilliant but wild, reckless with his impulses. He'll find his way, perhaps, but not here. The company would devour him before he ever got his footing.

Vivienne—I have always cared for her. She is Robert's by blood, mine by choice. But marriage has pulled her into another alliance, one I cannot trust. Her husband's name circles in whispers—questionable dealings, shortcuts, favors bartered. I can't prove it, but the timing of the board's sudden fixation on Ezra's bachelorhood… it felt engineered. Too sharp, too pointed to be coincidence. If Vivienne's husband saw opportunity in making Ezra appear vulnerable, I wouldn't put it past him to fan the flames.

And Vivienne, devoted as she is, might never see the knife until it's in her back.

Ezra, then, must be the fortress. My proof. My focus. My only bet.

That is why I called on Noelle Collins.

Not because I believe Ezra will suddenly fall in love like a storybook hero—I am not naïve. But because Noelle has the reputation to deliver what appearances demand. She is refined, capable, respected by women I respect. She has walked into rooms where no one wanted her there and left with their respect and trust anyway. If she can do that, she can stand toe-to-toe with Ezra.

But I will not leave this to chance. Not with the timeline pressing in, not with whispers gathering, not with years slipping faster than I ever imagined.

The doctors' words still echo—clinical, merciless. A few years. Perhaps more, perhaps less. My children don't know. To them, I remain indestructible. And I will let them believe it. But the truth stalks me in the quiet: my body is no longer the stronghold it once was. One day soon, I will not be here to silence the whispers before they reach the boardroom.

That is why failure is not an option. Ezra must be secure—optically, politically, personally. His position must be unassailable before I draw my last breath. I won't allow history to circle back and devour what we bled to build.

I turned my gaze to the city lights streaking past, my reflection faint in the glass. Ezra doesn't understand why I press so hard. He thinks my fixation on appearances is meddling. But he didn't live what I lived. He didn't watch the family legacy nearly slip from our hands.

I touched the pearls at my throat, cool and grounding. Ezra is my life's work, the culmination of everything Robert and I protected. And if Noelle Collins is as sharp as I've been told, perhaps she can help me ensure not just his survival, but his strength.

Because I will not watch my son fall. Ever..

CHAPTER 5

Fractures and Flickers

Noelle

Noelle settled back in her chair, headset snug at her ear. "All right, Valeria. Tell me everything."

Laughter bubbled through the line, bright and fizzy. "Everything? Then cancel the rest of your day, darling—it was perfect."

Noelle smiled, opening the file. "Start at the beginning."

"First of all—he had a driver. Not a car service. A driver. Door held open, chilled water waiting. Then Musaafer— private alcove, velvet drapes, carved wood. The sommelier practically sang when he poured the wine."

Noelle made a note, her voice even. "And the food?"

"Delicious, of course. But that wasn't it." Valeria's voice softened, a little breathless. "He made me laugh. Really laugh. He told this story about trying to impress a client in Tokyo and accidentally ordering a platter of raw wasabi leaves because he thought it was garnish. I nearly choked. My makeup artist would've killed me if she saw me laughing that hard, but I couldn't help it."

Noelle smirked. There it was. "That sounds like chemistry."

"It was." Valeria hesitated, her tone shifting. "But honestly? The best part wasn't dinner. When we left, I remembered I'd parked my own car down the block. He didn't just nod and get into his own—he walked me there. Held my umbrella. Waited until I was inside, the engine was running and I drove away. It was… small. Simple. But I felt—safe. Like someone was actually watching out for me."

Noelle let a beat of quiet hold, then said gently, "That's what matters. The velvet and wine fade. You won't remember the bottle next year. But the laughter, the umbrella—that stays."

On the other end, Valeria let out a softer laugh, this one carrying relief. "You're right. That's exactly what I kept thinking about."

"That's the point," Noelle said. "Not curating another fancy night. Building the kind of rhythm that lasts when no one's looking."

Valeria exhaled, lighter now. "He asked for a second date. I know he's only the second person you've introduced to me, but we really hit it off."

"Then you should go," Noelle said simply.

When the call ended, she wrote in clean black ink across the top of the file:
Green spark confirmed. Set up second date.

And for a moment, before reaching for the next folder, Noelle allowed herself a quiet smile. Not because the match was progressing—because she'd been reminded, again, why she believed in this work at all.

***

After Valeria's laughter faded from the line, I set her file aside, still wearing the faint echo of a smile. A knock at the door broke the quiet. Sadie stepped in, tablet in hand.

"Ezra Sinclair is here," she said.

I glanced at the clock. **Three o'clock, on the dot.** I'd braced for another show of power; instead, he arrived at the exact second I'd set. The fact that he'd adjusted at all sent a ripple through my composure I refused to show.

His suit was midnight navy with a subtle sheen, the fabric catching light like still water. The knot at his throat was crisp, exact. He moved with the kind of stride that didn't simply enter a room but recalibrated it, as though my office had been waiting for him.

"On time," I said before I could stop myself. Surprise slipped a shade too clearly into my voice.

He dropped into the chair opposite mine, faintly amused. "I figured if I showed up late again, you'd throw me out before I sat down."

I arched a brow. "You're absolutely correct."

A short breath escaped him—something close to a laugh, though he'd never call it that. Then he leaned back just enough to signal he was ready. "So. What do you have for me, Ms. Collins?"

I slid a leather portfolio across the desk. "Your personal branding session. A baseline—two places you actually relax, one story you've never put on a résumé, and what makes you laugh."

His lips tilted again, a sharper line this time. "This is where you tell me what tie to wear, what wine to order, how not to bore a woman out of her mind?"

"Actually, no. I don't tell my clients to put on a show," I said, smoothing the first page. "I heighten what's already there. If they let me."

His eyes didn't waver. Dark, steady, too intent. I'd stared down CEOs and senators who thought intimidation was strategy. But Ezra's gaze wasn't a test—it was a search, as if he wanted to see what I'd give away if I stayed in his line of fire too long.

"And what do you see here, when you look at me, Ms. Collins?"

Bait. He knew it. So did I. Still, I let my eyes sweep over him—slow, fully taking him in. The fabric of his suit stretched over muscle with the precision of bespoke tailoring. His watch—unassuming in design, obscene in price—glinted at his wrist. His body read like a man trained for mastery, not comfort. Beneath it was pressure—control gripped too tightly. He wanted the world to see him holding it all together. I saw the strain under the control, wire-taut.

I let the silence sharpen before I spoke, pen balanced between my fingers. "I see a man who mistakes power for warmth. That might close a deal, but across a dinner table? It feels like she's interviewing her financial advisor, not falling in love."

Something shifted in his expression. Not anger. Not offense. His eyes narrowed, gleaming like cut glass. A challenge. Mischief tugged at his mouth. He leaned forward, closing the inches between us—close enough for heat to roll off him.

"Warm enough?"

The air went heavy. His gaze cut once to my mouth, then returned to my eyes. My pulse betrayed me—quick, too quick—but I didn't move.

I tilted my chin and met his stare, refusing to yield. "You'll have to do better than that," I said, voice even though my breath caught sharp in my chest. "Now take your seat, Mr. Sinclair."

His smirk deepened—provocation refined to interest. He sat again, movements precise. The space between us hummed, a live wire.

I forced my eyes to the portfolio, pen biting harder against the page than I realized. "So. What makes you laugh?"

For once, he didn't answer right away. His gaze stayed locked, weighing me. Finally, his mouth curved, faint and private. "Dry humor. Old comedies. Watching people underestimate me."

"That last one wasn't funny."

"It is to me." The smirk returned, deeper.

I noted it, my hand less steady than usual. "Ruthless, with a side of sarcasm. Very marketable."

His eyes dipped to the page, then back to me, sharper. "And you? What makes you laugh?"

The question knocked me off balance. Clients rarely reversed the prompt. I hesitated, then said carefully, "Witty banter. Men who don't take themselves too seriously."

His gaze lingered, as though parsing layers I hadn't meant to reveal. Then he smiled again, slower this time. "So, anyone but me."

Heat rose in my cheeks anyway. "Exactly. Which is why you need me."

"Or maybe it means I've already gotten further than you expected."

The words landed too close, fire flaring low in my chest. I had a retort—but it stuck. He saw it. Of course he did. The silence that followed wasn't empty. It thrummed.

"I'll let you get back to what you were doing," he said, voice low, rich, clinging.

I lifted my chin, forcing coolness into my tone. "Do that."

Ezra stood, smoothing his lapel. He touched the portfolio with two fingers, aligning it to my desk's grid. Then he began walking towards the door. His hand paused on the brass handle a fraction longer than necessary. "Same time Friday?"

"Yes."

"I'll be on time."

His hand lingered—as though he'd leave if I let him, or stay if I asked. Then he turned the handle and left.

The door clicked shut, and the silence left behind felt heavier than the conversation itself. I stayed seated, pen still balanced between my fingers, staring at the closed door longer than I should have. My breath came shallow, my body strung tight.

Finally, I exhaled, set the portfolio aside, and reminded myself to stay professional.

But the room still held the charge to say otherwise.

***

Ezra

The elevator doors slid shut, and for the first time all day, my head wasn't on numbers or board politics. It was on her.

I'd walked into her office at the exact minute she set. That detail keeps needling at me now, the hum of the descent wrapping around it like static. I don't adjust for anyone—ever. Not for billion-dollar partners who clear their calendars. Not for politicians waiting on my arrival. My life moves when I say it does. Yet I walked through her door on her clock.

Not out of courtesy or respect. Out of something worse. I wanted to.

And I don't tolerate wanting. It's weakness.

That irritation carried me in, but it wasn't enough to stop me from leaning closer. A test, that's all. Close the distance, see if she broke. Most people do. They look away. They laugh too quickly, smile too brightly, fold themselves smaller without realizing it. That's how power works—you don't have to demand it. You just take the air out of the room until no one else can breathe.

But she didn't fold. Not once. Up close, her gaze stayed unflinching. I caught the faint lift of her breath—proof she felt it—but she held the line. And her mouth… there was the smallest curve there. Not a smile. Something sharper. Like she knew exactly what I was doing—and had already decided I wouldn't win.

That should've been the point I pulled back. That's control. You move away on your terms. But instead, I stayed. Pressed harder. And then—she told me to sit. Calm. Certain. Her tone carried no doubt, no nerves.

And I sat.

Now, floor by floor, the memory plays back. Not her words, but what lied between them. The heat threading between us, heavier than it should've been. My pulse climbing, not because she rattled me—but because I let the moment stretch. Because I didn't want it to end.

That's the problem. I know leverage when I feel it. And for one second in that office, she had it. That's what unsettles me. Not her beauty, though it's undeniable. Not her wit, though it cuts clean. It's the fact that—for the first time in years—I didn't care about walking away with the upper hand. I wanted to stay in her line of fire.

Which means this has to move quickly. Collins can set the introductions, I'll endure the dinners, tick the boxes, deliver the image the board demands, and close the file. Efficiency. Control. Done.

At least, that's the story I keep rehearsing.

But as the elevator slowed, the truth pressed harder, sharper: do I even want it done?

The bell chimed. The doors slid open to gleaming marble, light flooding in from the lobby. I straightened my jacket, mask back in place. To anyone watching, nothing had changed.

But I knew better.

Something broke open in that office. Something I didn't plan for. And when the time comes, I'm not sure if I'll stop it.

CHAPTER 6

Echoes of Silence

Noelle

Sadie walked into my office, eyes bright but cautious. "Your next client's here," she said softly. "Mr. Callahan. The widower I told you about."

"Send him in," I said.

Sadie nodded and disappeared.

A moment later, Mr. Callahan entered. Presence followed him—not the cultivated polish of men who lived for image, but something quieter, heavier. He was tall, his shoulders bearing a slight stoop that spoke of years of carrying weight that never fully lifted. His salt-and-pepper hair was neatly trimmed, his suit tailored but not ostentatious. He looked like a man who had once known exactly where he belonged in the world, and then lost it.

He offered a smile, polite and uncertain, the kind that flickered like a match struck in the dark.
"Ms. Collins. Thank you for seeing me."

"Please," I said, gesturing toward the chair across from me. "And it's Noelle. I'm glad you came."

He sat, folding his hands, silence pressing between us as though he was measuring whether his story had a place in this room. I let it breathe. Sometimes the silence was the first part of a long awaited release.

Finally, he spoke. "I lost my wife Margaret six years ago." His voice was low, steady, but reverent, like her memory was still a living presence. "We were married thirty-one years. High school sweethearts. She was my whole world." His throat caught, the edges of his composure fraying, but he pushed on. "I never thought I'd want to try again. But lately, I keep thinking she'd be disappointed if I didn't. Life's been… quiet. Too quiet."

The way he said *my whole world* softened something in me. I admired it—not just the span of years but the depth of them. A man who had loved so fully, so unapologetically, that her absence was still echoing through him six years later. That wasn't weakness. That was strength most people spent their lives pretending they didn't need.

"You had something very special," I said gently. "Loving someone that completely doesn't vanish when they're gone. It stays with you. And the fact that you're here now—choosing to open yourself again—that doesn't diminish her. It honors her."

His shoulders shifted, loosening a fraction, his eyes glistening as though my words pressed against something still tender. "I don't even know what I'm looking for. Someone kind. Genuine. I've built a company—software, tech—but that doesn't fill the house at night. Doesn't make the silence any less sharp."

I nodded, the ache in his voice resonating with something personal. My own bed often felt sharp too—cold sheets, dinner alone, silence that I filled with work. But unlike me, this man carried proof of what real love could be. Everlasting.

"You don't need to have the answers today," I told him. "That's what I'm here for—to help uncover them. To guide you toward something possible. You'll never replace what you had, and you shouldn't. But you can create something new. Something that honors both where you've been and where you're going."

For the first time, a smile briefly crossed his face. Small, tentative, but genuine. "You make it sound possible."

"It is," I said, meaning every word. "It's not about forgetting her. It's about building a future she'd be proud you chose."

He swallowed hard, eyes shining now, but his nod carried weight. "Then I'm ready."

I made a note in his file, but my hand lingered longer than usual. Admiration stirred in me—for him, for her, for a love that could last decades and still echo this loudly.

Ezra Sinclair might call marriage nothing more than a merger. But here was proof, sitting across from me, that love was more than survival. That it could be a force strong enough to outlive even death.

"Let's get started," I said softly, already determined to help him not just find companionship, but the courage to step toward life again.

***

Mr. Callahan's words lingered long after he left my office. *My whole world.* The way he said it—reverent, unashamed, carrying the weight of thirty-one years of love—struck something deep. He wasn't shackled by grief; he was honoring devotion. And in that honoring, he reminded me of what I wanted too. Not curated infatuations or glossy "couple goals," but the kind of loyalty that anchors, endures, and still echoes decades later.

The thought of going home to reheated leftovers and a hollow townhouse felt unbearable. Solitude as my only witness—tonight, that wasn't enough. Tonight, I needed to remind myself that romance wasn't only for my clients with portfolios and proposals. It was for me too. Even if the chair across from mine stayed empty, I would claim it—a quiet defiance against loneliness, a promise that one day it wouldn't be.

Sadie had wrinkled her nose when I asked her to book the reservation. *"You really want to sit in some fancy restaurant by yourself? People will stare."*
Yes. That was the point.

The maître d' greeted me by name and led me to a corner table overlooking the skyline. Chandeliers glimmered in the glass, the city pulsed beyond. Around me, the buzz of anniversaries, first dates, even a proposal three tables over. I ordered a Bordeaux and let myself breathe.

Rosemary bread arrived warm, fragrant. I tore off a piece, savoring it, letting myself simply be. No files. No clients. Just Noelle.

But silence has edges. It left space for thoughts I usually drowned in work. Greg's name rose like smoke—his four-word text still sat unanswered in my phone: *How've you been?* As if that could erase months of absence. Greg hadn't wanted me. He'd wanted the *idea* of a wife. Never again.

Halfway through my scallops, my phone buzzed. Ezra Sinclair's name lit the screen—just a calendar reminder Sadie had scheduled: Follow-up session, Wednesday. My pulse skipped anyway. Ugh. I set the phone facedown and pushed the plate aside.

Ezra Sinclair had no place in my personal thoughts, otherwise he'd become a liability. And yet his voice lingered, low and unyielding, curling through memory in ways I hadn't asked for.

I exhaled slowly, eyes on the skyline. *Romance yourself, Noelle.* That's what I always told my clients afraid to try again. Choose softness for yourself first. Believe you're worthy, even if no one's watching.

By the time I signed the check and stepped back into the night, Houston wrapped me in its glow. My heels clicked against the pavement, the rhythm I'd perfected. But beneath it pulsed a quieter truth:

I was tired of being powerful and alone.
And though I'd never say it out loud, I wanted—just once—someone who could meet me in both.

CHAPTER 7

A Match or a Mirror?

Noelle

I studied the profile glowing on my tablet, stylus tapping lightly against the glass. Every line gleamed—Harvard Law, high-stakes litigation, a board seat or two for good measure. Claudia Reyes. Accomplished, ambitious, the kind of woman who wouldn't flinch at Ezra Sinclair's stare. On paper, she was everything he claimed to value: credentials, legacy, stability. A mirror of his world, neat enough to hang in a frame.

"Interesting choice?" Sadie's voice floated from the doorway, threaded with curiosity. She knew me well enough to recognize I didn't pick names at random.

"Impeccable," I said, scrolling once more before closing the file. "She doesn't need Ezra's name to validate her own. And she wouldn't bend just because he pushes." I allowed myself a small nod. "That matters."

Sadie folded her arms, studying me. "And personally?"

I smiled faintly, keeping the truth tucked close. "Personally, she's the exact test he deserves. He says résumés matter more than chemistry? Then let's give him one that breathes—everything he claims is essential, standing across the table. Let's see if he notices what's missing."

Sadie didn't press. She trusted my instincts, even when she liked poking at them.

***

The next afternoon, Sadie announced Ezra's arrival for his first pre-date meeting. I'd already chosen Claudia Reyes. But Ezra wouldn't take what he was handed. He needed to believe the choice was his. So I staged the board: Anna Patel first, a strategic prelude.

When he walked in, steady as a storm front, he didn't sit. He prowled. His jacket pulled on his arms as though the fabric resented containing him, before he finally lowered himself into the chair opposite mine.

"You're scowling," he observed, voice flat but amused.

"Occupational hazard," I replied, sliding a folder across the desk. "Anna Patel. Former venture capitalist, now running a philanthropic foundation. Sharp, compassionate, grounded. She understands power but doesn't dwell in it."

He didn't glance. One long finger pushed the folder back toward me. "No."

"That was fast."

"I don't need to read her résumé to know she's not a fit."

"You don't need to…?" I let the words hang. "That's how this works, Mr. Sinclair. You read. You consider. You give it a chance."

"I don't waste time," he clipped. "Philanthropy is an ego stroke dressed as virtue."

I leaned back, folding my arms. "Or perspective. Something you could use."

A faint smile tugged at his mouth—provocation sharpened to a blade. "You think you know what I need?"

"I know more than you do," I countered.

His laugh was low, humorless. "Careful, Ms. Collins. That felt a little personal."

I tapped the stylus against my tablet. "I don't make it personal. I make it effective. And again—you came to *me* for a reason. So cooperate and let me do my job."

His gaze hardened, glinting. "Don't flatter yourself. I came because my mother boxed me in."

"Then you should thank her," I said sweetly, sliding Anna's file aside and lifting another. "Because without me, you'd still be at the office all alone, pretending graphs and tables can keep you warm at night."

That landed. His jaw flickered before he leaned forward, elbows braced, eyes unrelenting. "So what's next? Surely you have better than that."

"Claudia Reyes," I said, placing the second folder between us like a queen in a chess game.

This time, he moved. He flipped it open, scanning the record inside. Harvard Law. Senior partner before forty. Litigation wins stacked like trophies. Legacy background. A résumé strong as steel.

His brow lifted. "So my punishment for being late is dinner with a lawyer version of myself in heels?"

"Not yourself," I corrected, lips curving. "Your equal. Brilliant. Ambitious. Formidable. You said paperwork mattered, Mr. Sinclair." I tapped the file, "Claudia is paperwork in flesh and bone."

His mouth twitched, caught between smirk and smile. "Do you always weaponize people's words?"

I smiled as I shrugged, "Only when they're used carelessly."

The silence thickened. His thumb lingered on Claudia's photo longer than necessary before his eyes cut back to mine.

"And personally?" he asked.

I blinked. "Personally?"

"Yes. Do you like her?"

I held his gaze. "Personally, I think she's the perfect first date for you."

A slow curve touched his mouth. "Hmm. Perfect you say."

"Close enough anyway," I said, though my pulse betrayed me.

His smile sharpened. "Then let's see how good you really are."

He snapped the folder shut, rose, and adjusted his jacket. "Tomorrow night. I'll play along."

"Take it seriously," I murmured.

"Don't hold your breath."

He left in a sweep of cologne and command, his absence pressing against the walls long after the door closed.

And for the first time all day, it wasn't Claudia Reyes I was thinking about. It was the man who turned my carefully set board into a game—and made me wonder if I was playing it, or if he was playing me.

CHAPTER 8

Trial by Fire

Ezra

The restaurant was a thoughtful choice. White tablecloths pressed so tight they could've cut glass, a jazz trio tucked into the corner playing low enough to bleed into the clink of crystal. The air smelled of truffle and seared steak. Collins had picked well—elegant enough to impress, discreet enough to lower defenses.

Claudia Reyes was already seated when I arrived. Back straight, smile calibrated, her handshake measured down to the ounce.

"Mr. Sinclair," she greeted, rising a fraction before settling back. "When Noelle called, I wasn't sure what to expect. But here we are."

"Here we are." I took my chair.

She lifted her wine with the poise of someone who'd practiced the move for decades. "This place is a favorite. Fun Fact, the chef nearly lost his name in a licensing fight—I handled it. He still sends me risotto when I come."

"Good to have connections."

"Better to win them." Her smile cut a little sharper.

The cadence turned prosecutorial—carefully selected statements stacking like exhibits. "I just wrapped Reyes v. Edison Tech," she said. "They tried to bury us in motions. We didn't give them the chance."

I let the burn of my scotch linger. "Congratulations."

"Forbes called me 'the future of corporate litigation.' At thirty-nine, I'll take that." She gave a practiced laugh. Her plate untouched. Fifteen minutes gone. My replies clipped to courtesies.

She dabbed her mouth, pivoting. "But enough about me. Sinclair Holdings has been everywhere. The Riviera deal— brilliant. You'll own that market for a decade." She leaned in, lashes lowered; the compliment folded into flirtation. "How did you structure that acquisition? Personally involved—or delegated?"

Flattery masked as curiosity.

I rolled the glass between my fingers, light fracturing against the cut crystal. "Delegation. I don't sit in meetings I don't need to."

Her laugh went a shade too bright. "Efficient. I admire that. Though sometimes I imagine you miss the thrill of the chase."

A ghost of a smile. "Thrill fades. Results remain."

She searched for a crack. Finding none, she brightened as if she'd reached the real point. "My nonprofit's my passion. We raised nearly three million for educational equity this year. Senator Brown sat at my table—asked me to run. I told him I'd rather cross-examine than kiss babies."

I slid my phone out of my pocket, scrolling until I landed on Collin's name.

"Tell me this is your idea of a joke."

"She's billing me by the hour and forgot I didn't hire her."

Claudia laughed at her own line, pleased, and kept going. I nodded once—the kind of nod that meant present but detached.

By the forty-five–minute mark my verdict was clear. Brilliant. Accomplished. And utterly, painfully dull.

She laughed again, louder, and I thumbed a message.

"Flawless on paper. Chemistry nonexistent."

My thumb hesitated. Against better judgment I added—

"I guess I need a little more than paperwork."

Send.

I set the phone facedown, drained my glass, and let Claudia's voice recede into background hum. She was everything Collins had promised—but I didn't want her. In fact, all I felt was the urge to leave.

Damn Collins. She'd slipped past my guard without being in the room. Not with romance. With leverage. I pictured her writing her notes and psychoanalyzing me. Claudia's laugh cut again, too loud for a room like this. I raised my glass, expression smooth, thoughts elsewhere. This was only the first date. And already Collins had the upper hand.

***

The car door shut behind me, cutting off the restaurant's cultivated clatter. Silence pooled, heavy and welcome. I loosened my tie and my phone buzzed.

Noelle Collins: Call me when it's over.

A smirk. Of course. She never let me have the last word.

I dialed her number and she answered on the first ring.

"I believe," she said, low and edged with satisfaction, "you just admitted I was right, which means you were wrong."

I leaned into the leather. "I might've been… distracted."

Her laugh, soft and surgical. "Distracted enough to text me in the middle of a date with a woman who checks every box."

"She recited her résumé like I was interviewing her," I said. "I don't know anything about her I couldn't read on her website. No chemistry."

"And you didn't like that."

"No." The word scraped out rougher than I meant. "I didn't."

Silence stretched—taut, alive.

"Then will you let me do my job, Mr. Sinclair?" she asked, velvet over steel. "Because it sounds like, for once, you're ready for something real."

I let the pause linger. "Hmm. You sound awfully sure of yourself."

"I have to be. Someone has to counterbalance your arrogance."

A smile escaped me before I stopped it. "What you call arrogance keeps me undefeated."

"No," she said. "It keeps you a bachelor."

Her words landed harder than I cared to admit. I stared at the city lights bleeding past the tinted glass, phone hot in my hand, pulse uneven.

"Goodnight, Mr. Sinclair," she said finally, the tone smoothing back to business but threaded with something softer. "We'll be in touch about your next introduction."

The line clicked dead.

I sat in the dark car, tie undone, silence thick. Not Claudia's accolades circling back. Not her curated laugh.

Hers.

Always hers.

CHAPTER 9

Hollow Victories

Noelle

Ezra was finally learning he isn't bigger than the program. Software can sort résumés; I know how to spark fire. And I've been right too many times for anyone to call it luck.

Still, he kept sliding into my thoughts—the way he filled a doorway, the strength in his presence. A man with confidence does something to me, especially when he doesn't let it stand in the way of admitting when he's wrong. He gave off grown man energy.

I've got to focus. Ezra Sinclair is a file and I have to stick to my rules.

I set my phone on the marble console and drifted barefoot through the townhouse. The space held everything I once promised myself: art on the walls, lilies perfuming the air, candles in clean symmetry. Proof I could build a life worth living with my own hands.

Tonight the quiet pressed a little too close.

I poured wine and let Sade soften the corners of the room. The lilies breathed green and sweet while last night's Thai turned in the microwave. I ate at the counter, scrolling through client updates: a Cabo honeymoon, a Paris proposal, a note that read, *We never thought it was possible until you.* Their joy was my craft. My certainty.

And yet, when the glass ran dry and the playlist looped, his voice stayed low in my chest, uninvited.

Upstairs, steam blurred the mirror until I was only outline and breath. Cleanser, serum, cream—the small rituals that anchor me when the bigger things wobble.

I slid into bed, silk cool against my skin, lamplight pooling on the duvet. The other pillow lay untouched. My hand found the phone before I could talk myself out of it.

Greg.

The message had waited for days: *Hey. How've you been?*

I stared at it until the screen dimmed and woke again. We were good once—easy, even. Sunday markets and takeout on the floor. His palm at the small of my back in crowded rooms. He'd fix a door hinge at midnight because I'd mentioned it squeaked. I liked us.

Then came the nudges that turned into pressure. *Cut your travel clients. Fewer evening consults. Be home more.* Greg, like Ezra, was used to getting his way; Greg wanted it at my expense. I should've seen it sooner.

My thumb hovered over the keyboard. I typed, *Hope you're well*, and deleted it. Too polite. I tried, *Please don't contact me again*, then backspaced. Too final for a night like this.

The memory of the DMs flashed across my mind—*You should know he's not being honest with you*—followed by the photos from the St. Regis and the time-stamped screenshots that matched his "late meetings." Embarrassment first, hot and mean. Then the confrontation, overwhelmingly painful. Then another message.

I set the phone down.

Then picked it up again.

He'd begged after. Said he was in therapy. Said he understood the harm. He sent a screenshot of appointments I never asked to see. Shayla called it proof theater; I called it too late. Still, the part of me that loves a clean plan wondered if repair had a version here.

I opened my camera roll. There we were at the Menil green—his head tipped back laughing, my sunglasses crooked, happiness unposed. Another: he's stirring a pot, wearing my apron like a joke, steam fogging the lens. My chest tightened against my better judgment.

I typed, *I hope therapy has helped*, and erased it. He would read that as an invitation.

I typed, *I'm not interested in rehashing*, and erased that too. It sounded like I was already in the ring.

The townhouse hummed—dishwasher cycling, Sade's *Is it a Crime* looping a second time. Loneliness doesn't ask questions; it offers shortcuts.

Maybe he did learn. Maybe trying again would be easier than being brave alone.

I hated that the thought made sense.

My thumb moved before I could talk myself out of it.

I've been good. Busy. And you?

The dots appeared instantly, pulsing like a heartbeat. Regret rose, quick and metallic.

I turned the phone facedown and slid deeper under the sheets. Tomorrow I'd be sharp again—the woman no one rattles.

Tonight, the win didn't warm the other side of the bed.

PART II

THE UNSPOKEN

CHAPTER 10

Through the Glass Tower

Ezra

The tower wears my last name in steel at the crown, a clean line against the heat. Floor over floor, ambition stacked until the city thins beneath it.

On the executive level the sound changes. It's quieter here—the kind that means people have already sat up straighter. Everyone knows whose office anchors the hall.

Houston stretches under my windows like a lit map. I don't pause for it. Views are decoration. My job is keeping the ground steady and the company stable.

A junior analyst steps into my path, papers clutched. I know his name—Ramon—because he stays late and never complains.

"The Bianchi deal—"

"Start in Milan," I say, skimming the top sheet. "Dallas can wait."

He nods, relieved. "Got it, Mr. Sinclair."

"Ramon," I called out. "You've got your kid's game tonight. Be there."

He smiles, happy I remembered. "Yes, sir." He disappears, walking faster but lighter.

Two more appear with a too-bright laptop and hopeful numbers. The screen reflects in the glass, turning the city into a spreadsheet.

"Cut the fluff," I tell them. "Make it honest."
They read the subtext—and peel off.

In the conference room, conversation dies on cue. I take the head of the table. A fingertip tap is enough. "Go."

Updates roll—leases, a launch, a partnership that's been highly anticipated. I direct without raising my voice: what stands, what falls, what needs time. No one enjoys this part. That's fine. I'm not paid to be enjoyed.

By the end the air loosens. Someone jokes that if we're going to keep everyone awake, we should brand our own coffee. Laughter lands. I let half a smile have the room and close the folder.

This part is simple: pressure, clarity, a team that knows I'll make the work better or I'll stop it. Respect here is built into the job.

Outside these walls, it's a different sport. The board likes stories almost as much as returns, and lately Malcolm Price—Vivienne's husband—has been everywhere. A few years older. Political. Camera-ready. He shakes hands like he's collecting signatures. He doesn't have my numbers; he has momentum and people who like being flattered.

I gather the folders. One shuts harder than I mean to; the sound carries. Heads lift, then drop.

My phone buzzes with a calendar alert: *Board meeting*. Running Sinclair Holdings isn't the hard part.

Keeping it is.

I press a palm flat to the glass on my way out. The city hums back, steady and indifferent. Warmth keeps you in a room; power only opens the door. I learned that at home long before I learned it here.

The hall is already quiet again when I start down it. People straighten. The ground holds. For now.

***

The boardroom was never neutral ground.

Half the faces around the mahogany table leaned toward me, expectant. Most trusted results, and I had delivered. But two leaned back, guarded — chasing appearances instead of performance.

And above all, every eye flicked to the far end of the table. To my father.

Robert Sinclair never presided with speeches. He didn't need to. Authority radiated from him, shaping the entire room. He had grew this empire. I ran it now, but his presence reminded everyone whose name still crowned the glass tower outside.

"Ezra." Charles Whitmore inclined his head. Old Houston oil money. Loyal to my father first, to me as long as the numbers held.

"Morning, Ezra," Margaret Ellis said briskly. She'd been here since my grandfather's time and had no patience for charm. She measured results, and I'd given her plenty.

Further down, Jonathan Pierce twirled his pen, already settled on the outcome he wanted. Ellen Davenport adjusted the pearls at her throat, her approval reserved for society-page stability. They were the ones quietly angling for Vivienne's husband, Malcolm — not for merit, but because he looked the part.

Richard Hale lounged in his seat, the eternal swing vote, waiting to see which way my father leaned.

And beside me, Julian sprawled — tie loose, expression irreverent. The board dismissed him. I didn't. He was sharper than they thought, and unlike them, his loyalty wasn't conditional.

"Shall we?" I said, taking my place at the head of the table.

Reports came first. Acquisitions, expansions, margins. Strong numbers — the best in years. Whitmore nodded. "An excellent quarter. Ezra's leadership has steadied this company. The results speak for themselves."

Ellis added, "Numbers matter more than optics. He's delivered."

But Pierce leaned forward, voice smooth as oil. "No one disputes the figures. But stability isn't only financial. Legacy and image matter too."

Davenport's smile tightened. "Vivienne and Malcolm have been highly involved and visible. They project stability. It reassures people."

Julian snorted. "If you want a family portrait, hire a photographer. If you want this company to keep growing, leave Ezra where he is."

A ripple of chuckles. Davenport's expression soured.

Malcolm's name lingered, slick as oil.

"He isn't a Sinclair," I said evenly. "He didn't rebuild this company. He hasn't carried it through setbacks and recoveries. I did. And I'll keep doing it."

Richard Hale spoke next, deceptively casual. "Appearances do matter. Ezra's thirty-five. Unmarried. Investors like stability at home as well as in the books. Malcolm offers that image."

Julian laughed outright. "So record-breaking quarters don't count unless he's got a wife in diamondsat his side?"

"Julian." Ellis's voice cracked like a gavel. "Enough."

He leaned back, unrepentant, eyes on me.

The silence broke with my father, Robert Sinclair's voice filled the room — calm, commanding, absolute.

"The company is not a photograph," he said. "Ezra has delivered. That is what keeps Sinclair Holdings standing."

He didn't raise his tone. He never had to. The shift was immediate. Davenport dropped her gaze. Pierce's pen slowed. Hale sat forward, recalculating.

Whitmore seized it. "I agree. Ezra's given us stability where it matters. That's what counts."

Murmurs fractured the room — allies resolute, dissenters stiff, the undecided falling quiet. Waiting for Dad's next move.

I leaned back, outwardly steady though my jaw ached with restraint. This wasn't about metrics. Not here. This was politics in tailored suits. And Malcolm's name surfaced too easily.

I snapped my folder shut, the crack slicing through the quiet.

Let them whisper. Let them circle.

I hadn't carried Sinclair Holdings this far to watch them hand it to a man who hadn't earned it.

Not while I sat in this chair.

Not while Robert Sinclair still sat at the head of this table.

*****

I shut my office door harder than I meant to. The echo ricocheted off glass and steel, too sharp for a space designed to gleam.

The office stretched in sleek, precise lines: floor-to-ceiling windows framing the skyline, steel beams catching the glow of recessed lighting, a desk of black walnut polished to a mirror. Below, Houston sprawled like a model city — headlights threading through arteries of concrete, towers bowing faintly in reflection. From up here, I could see everything. Own everything.

And still, it never felt like enough.

I tugged my tie loose, dropped into the leather chair, and stared at the horizon. The numbers had been solid. Better than solid. But in that boardroom, results never stood alone. Legacy. Appearances. My personal life dissected like a balance sheet.

I pressed my palms to the desk, pulse thrumming in my fingertips.

The door opened without a knock.

Julian.

He sauntered in like he owned the place — jacket slung over his shoulder, tie hanging loose, grin accompanied by mischievous eyes. He dropped into the chair across from me, stretching his legs like he'd been waiting all day for this moment.

"You look tight, man," he said, grin widening. "One more vein in that forehead and you'll terrify the interns downstairs."

I gave him a look. "Don't start."

"Just an observation." He leaned back, hands laced behind his head. "Davenport looked like she might slide right out of her chair when you cut her off. Classic Ezra."

I shook my head, pinching the bridge of my nose. "Whitmore and Ellis can back me all day, but to the rest of them? Doesn't matter what I deliver if I don't fit their picture of stability."

Julian tilted forward, grin easing into something softer. "Yeah, well, you handled it. Don't let them crawl in your head. Half of them just like the sound of their own voices."

I exhaled slowly. He wasn't wrong. Still, unease prickled under my skin, stubborn as static.

Julian's smirk returned. "But I will say—your face when Pierce dropped Malcolm's name? Man, you cut your eyes so hard I thought the guy might combust on the spot."

A laugh escaped me before I could stop it. Low. Brief. But real. "You're ridiculous."

"And you're wound tighter than a drum." He leaned forward, elbows braced on his knees. "Which is why you need a distraction. Lucky for you, I've got one."

I raised a brow. "Here we go."

"Join my pickleball league."

I stared. "Pickleball?"

"Yeah. Tuesday nights. Outdoor courts. Chill crowd." He spread his hands like he was pitching a merger. "You need to get out of this glass box before it swallows you whole."

"Absolutely not."

"Why not?"

"Because if I play, I'll win. And if I'm going to win, I'll have to practice. And I don't have time for practice."

Julian pointed at me like he'd scored. "Translation: you're scared I'll run circles around you."

I leveled him with a flat stare. "You?"

"Don't underestimate me, big bro." He dropped his voice to a conspiratorial whisper. "The league fears me."

I snorted. "The league pities you."

Julian slapped the armrest, laughing so hard he nearly slid from the chair. "See? That's it. Trash talk is half the game. You're already halfway in."

I shook my head, but the pressure in my chest had shifted, loosened. That was Julian's gift — walking into a room thick with politics and stripping it of its weight, reminding me I wasn't carrying it alone.

He stood, tugging his jacket on, still grinning. "Tuesday. Seven o'clock. Don't make me call Davenport. Pretty sure she's hiding a serious backhand."

"Get out of my office," I said, though my voice carried less bite than I intended.

He pointed on his way out. "I'll take that as a maybe."

The door clicked shut, and silence reclaimed the office. But it wasn't the same silence as before.
This one felt lighter.

CHAPTER 11

Collision Course

Ezra

I told myself I wasn't going.

All afternoon I hid behind contracts and calls, pretending I had better things to do than humor Julian's latest sidequest. But when the office went quiet, the silence pressed in. My reflection stared back from the glass—tie loose, jaw tight, the boardroom's weight still on my shoulders.

Julian's voice lingered anyway: *Trash talk's half the fun. You're already halfway in.*

Maybe I wanted to prove him wrong. Maybe I just needed noise. Either way, I pulled into the lot as the floodlights blinked on over the outdoor courts.

The sounds hit me first—the sharp pop of paddles, the squeak of sneakers, laughter rising effortless into the humid Houston air. It was… lighter here. No suits, no strategy. Just people moving, playing, sweating, not thinking about business or deadlines.

I slipped past the fence, adjusting the grip on the paddle Julian had shoved into my hand earlier. My eyes swept the courts, expecting to catch my brother already holding court, already talking trash.

But I froze.

She was here.

At the far court, she moved like I'd never seen her move. Curls pulled back, paddle flashing in her grip. Her skin glistened under the lights, a sheen of sweat tracing the slope of her arms, catching on the delicate line where her collarbone disappeared into fabric. The outfit—nothing extravagant, just a fitted tank and skirt—clung in ways that highlighted every curve, every shift of muscle. Not calculated, not strategic. Just natural. Hers.

And that was what unsettled me.

Across my desk, she was all polish and precision. Blazers, silk blouses, controlled gestures. The version she wanted the world to see. But here? Her body moved with a freedom I'd never associated with her. Spirals of laughter shook loose from her chest as easily as the curls escaping her hair tie. She lunged, missed a shot by an inch, then grinned wide enough for the whole court to see.

Her beauty wasn't staged for an audience. It was alive. Uncontained. And it drew me harder than anything carefully orchestrated ever could.

I felt it in my grip on the paddle, the bite of it cutting into my palm. A pulse in my jaw I couldn't unclench. I wasn't supposed to notice her curves, the strength in her legs, the way the light kissed the edge of her waist. I wasn't supposed to feel heat crawl up my chest at the sound of her laugh.

But I did.

And then I saw him.

The man across the net, grinning back like her laughter belonged to him. Like he'd earned it. Something sharp twisted in my chest, hotter than it should've been. Jealousy.

My body reacted before my mind could catch up. Shoulders squared. Grip tightened. Instinct screamed: step forward, close the distance, claim the air between us and stake my ground.

But what ground was mine to claim? None. I was tripping, plain and simple.

Still, I couldn't look away. I thought I'd come here for distraction. For a game. But the court, the players, even Julian's echo of a dare—all of it blurred at the edges.

All I saw was her.

And then Noelle turned, as if she felt me watching. Our eyes locked across the space, and the noise around us dimmed.

The air snapped taut, charged, impossible to ignore.

***

Noelle

The rec center courts weren't glamorous, but they were alive. String lights looped along the fences, buzzing faint against the warm night. A speaker near the benches played low R&B, weaving through the squeak of sneakers and the pop of paddles. From the lot, the food truck's barbecue smoke drifted in, mingling with Gatorade tang and the faint bite of sunscreen.

This was my place to breathe. To laugh too loud. To strip off the armor I wore in glass towers and silver-lettered offices.

Andre tossed me a paddle, his grin cocky as ever. Former military, now deep in tech intelligence—the kind of man who could pull a social security number from a bad selfie. Off the court, he was my secret weapon, running quiet background checks before clients ever hit my books. But here, he was just my partner in trash talk.

"Rule one," he said, spinning his paddle like a showman, "work brain off."

"Rule two," I shot back, catching it easily, "don't embarrass yourself in front of me."

Andre lobbed me a paddle, already smirking. "Look at your form. Don't embarrass yourself"

I caught it, arching a brow. "Please. You're the one on a hundred-percent military disability. Who knows if you've still got it, *old man*."

He barked a laugh, shaking his head. "Old man? I'm ten years older, not ancient. And this—" he tapped his knee brace with the paddle—"just means I'm twice as efficient."

"That's one way to spin busted knees," I shot back, tugging my curls into a tie.

"You keep talking, but when I smoke you tonight, don't blame the VA."

"Uh-huh. You keep believing your own hype."

I lunged for a return, missed by a mile.

That set him off, doubled over, while two college kids waiting on the next court snorted. This was how it always went—half banter, half rally, more laughter than scorekeeping.

"Focus, Noelle!" Andre teased, diving for the return.

"I *am* focused," I said, breathless from laughing as much as running. "On making sure you don't pull something trying to keep up with me."

He groaned like I'd insulted his honor, then missed a return, giving me the point. I pumped a fist in mock victory, soaking up the applause from the sidelines like I'd just won the U.S. Open.

"You're impossible," he muttered, grinning despite himself.

"And you love it," I tossed back, shoulder-bumping him before lining up for the next serve.

This was it. The version of me no one saw behind Collins & Co.—messy, competitive, laughing until my cheeks hurt. Not the matchmaker, not the strategist. Just me.

I lunged for a return, missed, and collapsed into a laugh that carried across the court. My curls were coming loose, sweat clung to my temples, and for once, I didn't care.

Then, mid-laugh, something made me glance toward the gate.

And froze.

Across the courts, tall and still in the shadows, eyes fixed on me.

Ezra Sinclair.

The paddle slipped in my hand. The music, the laughter, the night—it all thinned under the weight of that stare.

I didn't move. Neither did he.

And just like that, my sanctuary wasn't just mine anymore.

***

Ezra

I was ready to move. Ready to cross the court and make my presence known, if only to wipe that grin off the guy standing across from her.

But before I could take a step, the whistle blew.

"All right, people—let's split it up! Courts one and two, you're starting first. Pairs, let's go!"

The crowd shifted fast, bodies moving, voices calling out names. Teams rearranged, laughter spilling as paddles clacked against palms. Noelle turned away, swept up in the shuffle, and I was left standing still, paddle in hand, caught between wanting to follow and not sure how without looking like a fool.

"Ezra!"

Julian waved me over, already grinning like he'd won something. "You're with me. Court two."

Of course.

I stepped onto the court, the ground still hot from the day, floodlights cutting sharp angles across the paint. Across the net, two regulars I didn't know smirked at Julian like they'd been waiting for payback.

"You ready?" he asked, bouncing the ball in his palm.

"No."

He laughed, tossed me the serve. "Good. That means you'll actually try."

The game kicked off.

It was chaos from the start. Julian played like it was a comedy routine, cracking jokes between swings, pumping his fist every time we managed a point. I found myself locked in almost immediately, muscle memory from years of tennis and squash carrying me forward. Quick pivots, sharp smashes, clean serves—control where I could get it.

The sound of sneakers squeaking, the ball cracking against paddles, the rush of bodies moving—it was different from the office. There, silence was my weapon. Here, it was noise, laughter, shouts.

I hadn't realized how much I needed it until I was in it.

Julian whooped after a volley, nearly running into me. "That's what I'm talking about!".

And I didn't hate it. For a moment, it was freeing to finally let go and do something fun.

But then my eyes were drawn sideways to Noelle playing across the next court. Her hair had slipped free, curling at her temples, her cheeks flushed with heat. She swung—missed the ball by inches—and laughed. A real laugh, unguarded, bright enough to cut through everything else. Her partner teased her, she shoved his shoulder, grinning like she'd won anyway. Her beauty made it hard to look away.

Something cinched low and sudden inside me, as if the laugh had cut through armor I didn't know I still wore.

The ball smacked against my shoulder before I even saw it coming.

"Damn it, Ezra!" Julian barked, darting across to save the point. "Tighten up—we're supposed to be winning, not daydreaming!"

I rolled my shoulder, muttered something sharp under my breath, but my eyes betrayed me. They went back to her. And just then—hers found mine.

A glance. Quick. Electric. The kind that hooks before you can look away. Her smile lingered half a second too long before she turned back to her game. My pulse spiked like I'd just sprinted the length of the court.

"Focus!" Julian shoved past me, landing a clean point. "I can't carry your dead weight out here!"

I muttered something under my breath, rolling my shoulder. But my eyes had already betrayed me.

Because she was looking at me. Her smile softening, mine slipping in despite myself. The rest of the court fell away—the noise, the sweat, the chaos. Just her.

The game finally ended in our favor—narrowly—Julian crowing like he'd carried us when we both knew otherwise. We bumped paddles with our opponents, sweat-drenched and breathless, and as the crowd shifted again for the next round, I spotted Noelle slipping away toward the side benches—towel draped around her neck, water bottle in hand.

And this time, I didn't think twice.

I started toward her.

She was still catching her breath when I reached her, paddle braced against the bench. Sweat clung at her temples, but the flush across her skin was all adrenaline.

The guy beside her was still holding a paddle, grinning at something she'd said. He leaned in with the kind of familiarity and comfort you didn't fake.

I cleared my throat. Her eyes cut to me, sharp and unimpressed. "Of course you're here."

I smirked, tugging at the damp collar of my shirt. "What? Afraid I'll mess up your game?"

She arched a brow. "Callin it my game implies you have one. Pretty sure you just barely survived yours."

I let out a low laugh and dropped onto the bench beside her. Close enough to catch the faint citrus of her perfume under the night air.

"You talk a lot of trash for someone who couldn't keep the ball inbounds," I said.

The guy gave a low whistle, shaking his head. "I'll leave you two to it before I end up playing referee." He clapped her shoulder lightly, nodded once in my direction, and headed toward the water station.

The silence he left behind was louder than the laughter on the courts.

Her mouth curved, the beginnings of a smile she tried to hide. "Sounds like you were watching me."

"Hard not to." The words came before I could stop them, rougher than I intended.

Her eyes flickered, heat and challenge both sparking there. "Maybe you should focus on your own court next time."

"Maybe I liked the view better on yours."

That stopped her, just for a moment. Her lips parted, breath catching like she hadn't expected me to say it out loud. I almost regretted it—almost.

Before she could answer, Julian appeared, towel slung around his neck, grinning like he'd just walked into his favorite sitcom. "Ezra," he said, then tipped his chin toward Noelle. "who's your friend?"

Noelle straightened, her voice crisp, professional. "Noelle Collins."

Julian tilted his head, curious. "Noelle Collins. Right. But how do you two know each other?"

The air tightened. I could feel her about to sidestep, to keep it vague—*business acquaintances*, something safe enough to disappear behind.

But before she could, I heard myself say it.

"She's my matchmaker."

Julian's brows shot up, amusement sparking in his eyes. Noelle's head snapped toward me, her eyes sharp with shock before she smoothed it into cool composure. But I saw it—the flare of warning.

And as Julian's grin widened, I asked myself the question I already knew the answer to—why the hell hadn't I let her lie? Why had I just claimed her like that?

Before I could react, a voice called from across the lot: *"Noelle! You ready? Car's out front!"*

She slipped her paddle under her arm and rose, her composure flawless. "That's my ride." She gave Julian a polite nod, gave me nothing, then turned and quickly walked away.

I tracked her until she disappeared past the gates, jaw tight, heat crawling under my collar.

Julian let out a low chuckle beside me. "So that's her. Didn't think I'd see the day you needed a matchmaker." He leaned in just enough for only me to hear, voice slick. "She got under your skin, didn't she?"

My grip tightened on the paddle. I didn't answer.

He clapped my shoulder again, before peeling off toward the other courts, calling greetings like he hadn't just thrown a match into a room full of gasoline.

I stayed rooted on the bench, eyes fixed on the spot where she'd vanished.

And for the first time in a long while, silence didn't feel like control. It felt like a loss.

***

Noelle

The night air cooled nothing. Not the heat on my skin. Not the echo of his voice.

She's my matchmaker.

A line that should have slid clean. Just a fact. But the way he said it—steady, almost possessive—clung like a fingerprint

I couldn't wipe away. He could have brushed me off as a colleague, a contact, a service. Instead, he'd claimed me. And I hadn't corrected him.

Why?

I gripped the towel around my shoulders tighter as Andre fell into step beside me, paddle tucked under his arm, grin already trouble.

"Well, well," he drawled. "Looks like Mr. Sinclair's caught up."

I shot him a look. "Please. Ezra Sinclair doesn't get caught up. He came to me for a match with a powerful woman, remember?"

Andre chuckled, slow and knowing. "And you don't qualify?"

The question knocked me back a beat. "That's not the point. I'm not his anything. I'm his matchmaker."

"And yet," Andre said, tilting his head toward the courts we'd just left, "the man didn't take his eyes off you. Didn't even try to."

I forced a laugh, brushing it off like sweat at my neck. "You're imagining things."

"Mm." He hummed, unconvinced. "Funny thing about men like him—they don't announce their business in public. Not unless they want it known."

I turned away, sliding into the passenger seat of his car. The leather was cool against my legs, but my chest burned restless. I told myself it was the match, the adrenaline, the thick Houston air.

But the echo wouldn't quiet.

She's my matchmaker.

And what bothered me most wasn't the claim itself. It was the part of me—the quiet, inconvenient part—that almost wished he'd meant something else.

CHAPTER 12

The Ache of Ease

Noelle

Ezra Sinclair's file had taken over my kitchen table—profiles fanned out like a deck of cards, compatibility scores highlighted, notes scribbled in the margins. Normally, this part of the process calmed me. Matchmaking was a puzzle, and I was good at puzzles.

But tonight the pieces refused to lock in place.

His photo—dark suit, controlled stare, heir apparent stamped into every line—kept slipping into something else. The man on the pickleball courts. Shirt damp, jaw tight, eyes locking on mine like I'd caught him off guard. Like I wasn't supposed to get to him… but did.

I forced the thought away and flipped open my notes from his first date. Claudia Reyes.

On paper, Claudia had been flawless. Brilliant attorney. Classy. Background to match his own. She ticked every box. And yet, his verdict had been blunt: *Paperwork flawless. Chemistry nonexistent.*

I chewed on the cap of my pen, replaying the night. Claudia was sharp, confident, his equal in every measurable way—but she was too much like him. He'd sat through dinner detached, polite, already checked out. No curiosity. No challenge that unsettled him in the right way.

That was the problem. It wasn't enough to hand him someone impeccable. He needed someone who could push him—but also soften the edges. Someone who could meet him where he was and still pull him somewhere else.

I set Claudia's file aside and reached for the folder Evelyn had pressed into my hands earlier this week. *One of mine,* she'd said, her tone like a velvet hammer.

Elise Carrington.

Thirty-two, River Oaks. Old Houston money. Galas, charity boards, glossy magazine spreads. She ran her family's foundation and carried herself like a woman who'd never broken a sweat.

I'd vetted her, of course. Clean record. No scandals. Exactly the kind of woman Evelyn thought her son needed—

the kind who looked the part of stability.
And the kind Ezra would despise.

I could already picture it: Elise smiling warmly but rehearsed, telling practiced stories for donors, never once cracking the surface. Ezra checking his watch, sending me the same text.

Safe didn't work for Ezra Sinclair.

I pushed Elise aside and reached for one of mine.

Maya Thompson.

Thirty-three. MBA. Strategy manager at a Houston energy firm. Born into oil and gas money, but she hadn't coasted on the family name. She'd carved her own path—late nights, renewables, strategy over legacy. Colleagues described her as sharp, empathetic, the kind of leader who solved problems without cutting people down.

She had the air of someone raised around expectation, but the drive of someone determined to be more than a surname. Not Evelyn's choice. Not "safe." But real.

If Claudia had been too rigid and Elise too rehearsed, Maya was the balance. Steady, sharp, warm. The kind of woman Ezra might actually stay present with.

I tapped my pen against her profile, imagining his reaction—interested, maybe even impressed. She wasn't "perfect". But she was better.

I slid her folder to the top of the stack. "Date number two," I murmured.

Still, at the back of my mind, another image intruded. Ezra on that court, eyes fixed on me, his voice low: *Hard not to.*

I shoved the thought aside.

Maya Thompson was the right choice. She had to be.

I packed her folder into Ezra's file, shut the laptop, and tried to believe my own judgment.

***

By the time I pulled into my parents' driveway, twilight had folded itself over the street. The porch light glowed the way it always had when I was a teenager sneaking home late, roses climbing thick around the trellis. From the open kitchen window drifted the smell of cornbread and collard greens, rich and familiar.

Mom opened the door before I even reached it, dish towel still in hand. "About time," she said, pulling me into a hug hard enough to drop my shoulders. "You don't call enough. And you've lost weight."

I laughed into her shoulder. "Hi, Mom. Nice to see you too."

She kissed my cheek, then steered me straight toward the table. "Sit. Eat. That's the rule."

Dad followed with two sweating glasses of iced tea. He set one in front of me and gave me his usual half-smile. "Don't argue. It never works."

"Thirty-four years, and he still tries," Mom said, sliding a basket of cornbread between us.

"Thirty-four married," Dad corrected, easing into his chair. "Thirty-five together. I can't be that bad—remember you said yes after one year."

I shook my head, smiling despite myself. "Guess you knew early."

"Still do," he said simply, resting his hand on the back of her chair like it had always belonged there.

We ate at the same scarred table I'd grown up around, the wood edges worn smooth from decades of elbows and laughter. Conversation drifted the way it always did here—traffic on the loop, the neighbor's new dog, whether my brother, Cal, was working too much again.

"He calls, but he doesn't stop moving," Mom said, passing me the greens. "I can hear it in his voice—like he's walking laps while he talks."

Dad chuckled, low and steady. "That boy's always been restless. Don't take it personal."

Her hand lingered at her glass, thumb circling the rim. "Restless is one thing. The hours he keeps, the places he disappears to…" She let the thought fall away, as though saying it aloud would make it heavier.

"He takes care of himself," Dad said, quiet but firm enough to ease her shoulders. "Always has. You know how he does."

Mom studied him, and for a moment the air between them softened. His hand brushed a crumb from her cheek without thinking, and though she swatted at him, the curve of her mouth gave her away.

I found myself watching them more than eating—the tilt of her head when she laughed, the absent way his fingers stayed hooked at the back of her chair. Small gestures. A marriage lived out in details.

And it pulled me straight back to when my mom lost her hair, and my dad learned to tie her scarves the way she liked—soft cotton, careful knots. He lined up pill bottles on a saucer by color, drove every appointment, asked every question. He warmed soup, folded laundry, cracked bad jokes in waiting rooms, and slept upright in those impossible chairs because going home without her wasn't an option. It was always the two of them against the diagnosis, hand in hand, lifting each other up.

That's what I want. Someone who sees me, chooses my joy, and doesn't step back when it gets heavy. My parents were great at loving us because they loved each other first—their devotion spilled over, and we grew up in the overflow.

"You're quiet tonight," Mom said finally, looking at me over her glass.

"Work," I answered.

"Tough one?" Dad asked, his voice comforting, but his gaze saw right through me—the kind that made it hard to answer anything but honestly.

I nudged rice across my plate. "Something like that."

They didn't press. Just exchanged a look across the table, the kind I'd grown up seeing—half a conversation carried in silence.

After dinner, I dried while Mom washed and Dad stacked. Their fingers brushed in passing, small touches they probably didn't notice. She did, though. I caught the softness in her eyes each time.

I swallowed against the ache rising in my chest. This—this was what I wanted. The ease that settled after decades, quiet and unshakable.

And later, driving home under the weight of a sky gone dark, another image pushed in uninvited. Ezra Sinclair. His guarded stare, his walls. The man I'd just set up with Maya Thompson. A man who didn't believe in fairy tales. A man who might never believe in *this*.

My grip tightened on the wheel, knuckles sharp against the leather. I told myself to let it go. To shake him off.

But the thought stayed. Stubborn. Unwelcome. And impossibly alive.

CHAPTER 13

Better isn't Enough

Ezra

Maya Thompson was impressive.

Her file had been one of the few that stood out to me: strategy manager at a major energy firm, respected in her field, carved her own path. She'd built something real in a competitive industry, and I came today expecting to meet that woman.

The valet slid my bag from the trunk like it was a baton in a relay. Live oaks threw long fingers of shade across the drive; country clubs all smell the same—cut grass, sunscreen, old money—but this one added late-summer heat and the mineral bite of the sprinkler system coming on.

"Sinclair, party of two," the starter said, pencil behind his ear. "Cart's ready."

Maya stepped out from the portico in a pale-blue tank and visor, legs steady in golf shoes that had seen more than a few rounds. She moved like someone who'd grown up around places like this but didn't depend on them to feel legitimate.

"Mr. Sinclair," she said, offering a hand.

"Ezra," I corrected.

"Ezra," she repeated. "Thanks for meeting here. Thought it'd be good timing—it's usually quieter at dusk."

"Your file said you play."

A quick smile. "Play, not compete. I'm here to enjoy it."

I took the wheel because she gestured for it, and because control is a hard habit to break. The cart hummed; cicadas worked the tree line. Dusk had the fairways turned that deep, expensive green you only get with irrigation.

She pulled both a driver and three-wood, weighing them in her hands like a decision that had moral stakes. I waited. She looked over.

"What would you hit?" she asked.

"Whichever you'd hit if I weren't standing here."

She chose the three-wood, grinned faintly, then swung, and sent the ball sailing—safe. Respectable. Nowhere near the trees, nowhere near the water. I hit one harder, farther, more defiant than smart..

"Nice," I said.

"Margin for error," she answered, smile quick and private.

We rode in silence for a minute. The cart path crunched under the tires. Through the trees I could see the pool—kids launching cannonballs into a blue rectangle while their parents pretended not to notice.

"So," she said lightly, "last real vacation—what does that look like for you? Island or city?"

"Neither. Mountains," I said. "No reception."

"Perfect," she said immediately. "I love mountains. If you prefer…"

"You love mountains," I repeated. "Which ones?"

Her smile adjusted a millimeter. "Most of them. I'm flexible."

The words scratched at me. We played our approaches—hers tidy, mine aggressive. She asked, "What does an ideal Saturday look like for you?"

"You first."

She blinked, then recovered. "I'm not picky."

"Humor me."

"Coffee. Pilates. Errands." She glanced up for approval. "Dinner somewhere quiet. Unless you prefer loud."

"What's a hill you died on this month," I said, hitting a clean putt. "Not in theory."

She laughed softly, a careful sound. "I try not to die on hills. It's more effective to—"

"Pick one," I urged.

She set her putter down, thought, then lifted her chin. "Okay. People who say they 'don't believe in oil' while they Uber everywhere are hypocrites. If your choices don't match your ideals, they're just fiction."

"That," I said, "is the first thing you've said that wasn't waiting for my face."

"Is that…good?"

"It's true. I'll take true over agreeable."

Without asking, she reached into my bag and handed me the driver I favor, grip already turned the way I like it. Noted.

"How'd you know?" I asked.

"I read the Q&A you did for *Texas Business* last year," she said, voice steady but her ears warmed. "You mentioned your swing coach liked a heavier head."

It should have been flattering. Instead, it left me uneasy.

She steered everything back to me. What kind of woman I wanted. What kind of dinners I liked. Whether I preferred my future wife to stay home with the kids. She asked, she listened, she adjusted her smile like she was building a profile on me.

I knew she had opinions. She wouldn't be where she was without them. But here—across from me—she acted like sharing them might be too much, like being fully herself would cost her points.

I took another swing, masking the shift in my mood, and studied her more closely. Beautiful, elegant, a woman most men would be proud to bring to any dinner. But the version she showed me today was like a mirror—reflecting me back at myself instead of letting me see her.

Then came her laugh.

High, careful, practiced. The kind of sound that belonged at charity tables, smooth and perfectly inoffensive.

And before I could stop it, another laugh cut through my thoughts—Noelle's.

Sharp. Bright. Reckless enough to carry across the pickleball courts, uncurated, uncontained. A laugh that had jolted something in me I hadn't realized was waiting.

The difference between them was too stark. Maya's laugh skimmed the surface. Noelle's had driven straight through me.

Maya's hand brushed my sleeve, her eyes lifting like she was waiting for me to approve of her answer, her presence, her very way of sitting here with me.

I gave her the smile she wanted—polite, contained.

Inside, I already knew.

She wasn't showing me herself. And I don't want a woman who thinks the price of my life is hers.

***

Noelle

I stacked Maya Thompson's profile neatly on top of Ezra's file, pen poised to take notes. I should have felt hopeful. After Claudia, I needed this to work—needed him to tell me I'd gotten it right this time.

So when Ezra arrived—clean citrus and cedar trailing in with him—I forced my smile professional. "Mr. Sinclair. How was the evening?"

He sank into the chair across from me, stretching his legs like he owned the space, and let the silence breathe just long enough to make me feel it. Finally: "She seemed better."

Hope flared sharp in my chest. Better was progress. Better meant maybe, finally, this was working. I readied my pen. "Better than flawless Claudia? That's high praise."

He smirked—faint, deliberate. "She was good. Smart. Warm. The kind of woman my parents would approve of."

My stomach tightened. That was exactly what I should want to hear. That she would be acceptable to his parents. And yet… unease slid through me, hot and sour. Because the way he said it—the ease, the acknowledgment—it sounded too much like approval. Like he might actually have liked her.

"That's promising," I managed, though my grip on the pen was too tight.

His gaze locked in on me, heavier than the room could hold. "But she didn't hold me."

The pen slipped, a dark line bleeding across the margin. Relief rushed hot and dangerous through me, loosening something in my chest I had no business letting go. I should want Maya to succeed. I should want any of them to succeed. That was my job.

Instead, a traitorous whisper unfurled inside me: Thank God she didn't.

I cleared my throat and straightened, forcing composure. "Not every spark is immediate, Mr. Sinclair. Chemistry builds."

"Or it doesn't."

His words were measured, but the meaning pressed heavy between us. Against my better judgment, I met his eyes.

"Do you really believe that?" I asked, softer than I meant.

He leaned in, citrus and cedar winding across the desk. "I've believed a lot of things," he said quietly. "Some of them… I'm starting to question."

Heat rose in my throat. I tucked a curl behind my ear just to give my hands something to do. "About what?"

His eyes didn't waver. "About whether the things I thought mattered most actually do."

The air pulled taut, sharp as glass. My pulse thudded, the hum of the air conditioner suddenly too loud.

"You hired me to find you a match, Mr. Sinclair," I said, smoothing the papers just to brace myself. "Not to unravel your philosophy."

"Maybe the two aren't so different."

He wasn't teasing. His tone was too even, too certain. And the way his gaze lingered—too long, too heavy—made the air between us feel thick.

I reached for distance. "You sound like a man who doesn't know what he wants."

"Or maybe I sound like a man who's finally starting to."

The words hung between us, dangerous. His eyes flicked down—quick, unmistakable—to my mouth before finding mine again.

My breath hitched. I should have looked away. I didn't. The scrape of my pen against paper was forgotten. The silence stretched, charged, sparking in places I didn't dare name.

And then the knock shattered it.

My assistant poked her head in, oblivious to the storm she'd cut through. "Sorry to interrupt, Ms. Collins. Greg called to confirm your seven o'clock—said he's taking you to dinner?"

The name landed like a slap.

Ezra's jaw ticked, his stare snapping sharp to me.

Heat surged up my neck. "Thank you," I said quickly, thinner than I wanted. "I'll… be out shortly."

The door closed, but the quiet it left behind wasn't calm.

Ezra hadn't moved. His gaze stayed locked on me, dark and unreadable, before he rose. His mask slid back into place.

"Enjoy your evening, Ms. Collins." His voice was even, but edged.

He left without another word.

I sat frozen, pen useless in my hand, citrus and cedar still clinging to the air.

And for the first time since I'd opened this business, I wasn't sure if I wanted my client's match to succeed at all.

CHAPTER 14

In the Heat of the Night

Ezra

The air outside her office was thick with heat, the kind that clung even after sundown. I slid into the driver's seat, jaw tense, *Greg.... he's taking you to dinner* still echoing like a taunt. The words had landed in the room like a stone. I'd walked out composed, stride steady. But inside, I was fuming.

I sat there for a long moment, hands braced on the wheel, trying to force the irritation down. It wasn't jealousy. I didn't get jealous.

Except—maybe I did.

Movement pulled my eyes toward the lot. Noelle. Brisk steps, heels sharp against the pavement, posture all poise and armor. She carried herself like she could outrun the weight of the world if she had to. I told myself to look away. Drive off.

And then she stopped short.

Her head tilted, gaze dropping to the rear wheel. Even from here, I saw it—the sag in the rubber, the quick dip in her shoulders. Flat tire.

She didn't panic. Of course she didn't. Just irritation, clipped and contained. One hand went for her phone.

Before I realized it, my door was open.

She noticed me crossing the lot, eyes narrowing. "Don't tell me you just happen to be parked here."

"Don't flatter yourself." My tone was even, but we both knew better. My gaze flicked to the tire. "You're not driving on that."

"I'm calling roadside service." She scrolled, cool and efficient.

"Don't waste your time." I shrugged off my jacket, set it across her hood, and crouched by the wheel. "I'll handle it."

Her brows rose, sharp as her voice. "Handle it? As in—you?"

I looked up at her, briefly. "I know how to change a tire, Ms. Collins. Not everything requires a staff."

That left her speechless. For once.

The wrench was cool in my hand as I braced against it, sleeves rolled high, the humid night clinging to my skin. She crossed her arms, but her eyes stayed fixed—watching, measuring.

"Didn't picture you as the type to get your hands dirty," she said finally.

The steel gave with a sharp snap, bolts loosening one by one. "I know how to do a lot of things people don't picture."

Her gaze lingered.

The rhythm steadied me—jack, bolts, spare. Muscle memory. From the time I was a teenager, my father made sure I could handle work like this. Saturday mornings in the garage, grease under our nails, him swearing that a man should know how to take care of his own damn car before he thought about owning one. I hadn't touched a flat since college, but the motions came back clean, efficient. This was work that didn't need charm or strategy—just torque, sweat, control.

When I tightened the last lug and lowered the jack, I stood, dust streaking my palms, a smear of grease across my wrist. I pulled a handkerchief from my pocket, wiped once, then tossed it into the trunk before closing it with a snap.

"All set," I said simply.

She exhaled, softer than I expected. Almost surprised. "Thank you."

Two words. Unvarnished.

I slid back into my jacket, smoothing the lapels, composure restored with the motion. "Check the pressure this week. Don't wait until it costs you."

Her eyes flickered, something softer slipping through before she caught it.

I didn't give her the chance to answer. I turned, walked back to my car, slid behind the wheel.

By the time the engine purred to life, she was still standing there, arms loose now, still staring my way, expression unreadable in the wash of the streetlight.

I pulled out, steering toward the Sinclair estate. Toward dinner. Toward my mother's inevitable questions.

But the only thing I carried with me was the sound of her voice—quiet, certain, lingering longer than it should have.

Thank you.

CHAPTER 15

The Illusion of Control

Ezra

The wrought-iron gates slid open on a whisper, the long drive unfurling like a private runway cut through old trees and older money. Live oaks arched overhead, their branches braided into cathedral vaults, lanterns casting warm pools of light along the gravel's edge. The Sinclair estate wasn't just land—it was lore. Reporters used to joke it deserved its own zip code, and they weren't far off. Sixty acres carved from Houston soil, fenced in with iron and history, guarded not just by gates and cameras but by the weight of the name itself.

Everything here ran with military precision. Groundskeepers trimmed the oaks and bushes into perfection, housekeepers moved like shadows between the houses, Michelin star chefs. Weddings had been staged here, galas, political fundraisers. To the outside world, Sinclair Row wasn't just untouchable—it was myth made flesh.

Inside the gates, though, it was only us. My parents, my siblings, and me, each tucked into our corners like monarchs ruling separate provinces. Close enough to see each other's lights at night, far enough that the distance between us had stopped being measured in yards and started being measured in years.

Julian's place came first, loud even in silence—modern glass half-hidden behind the oaks, a basketball hoop planted in the drive, music always pulsing through the walls. Vivienne's house stood farther in, symmetrical brick and white columns, every shutter aligned like soldiers. Malcolm's car was parked in plain sight, as if announcing his arrival.

Mine sat last, tucked behind a bend of trees. Dark limestone, clean steel lines, built to hold silence without feeling empty.

I pulled into the garage, the door closing behind me with its familiar hum. My tie was still loose, cuffs still smudged with faint streaks of grease.

I could've called someone. There were drivers, valets, staff on retainer who would've handled a flat in minutes. That was the way things worked now—problems passed off, solutions delivered.

But tonight, I hadn't wanted anyone else. I wanted it to be me. Her flat tire, her clipped irritation softening just enough when she said it. *Thank you.* Two words that carried more weight than they should have.

The shower ran hot enough to scour the grease from my wrists, steam rising until the mirror blurred. Still, she lingered. The sharp laugh on the courts, the way her shoulders had loosened tonight, like she'd let herself put the weight down—if only for a moment.

I braced my palms against the tile, letting the sting ground me.

When I finally dressed again, the house felt colder. Watch clasped, cufflinks fastened, I crossed to the dresser. An old photo leaned against the wall: me, Julian, and Vivienne at a county fair, faces smeared with powdered sugar from funnel cakes, grins wide and careless. Back then, we weren't proving anything. We weren't carrying names, or empires, or expectations. We were just kids in the sun.

I straightened the frame before heading out.

The path to the main house stretched ahead, hedges clipped into perfect symmetry, lanterns glowing steady. Dinner waited. Questions would too.

But what followed me through the night wasn't the weight of legacy.
It was her voice—smooth, certain, still clinging like smoke.

Thank you.

***

Hector pulled the front door open before I reached it. "Evening, Mr. Ezra."

"Evening," I said, stepping into the familiar blend of lemon oil and magnolia that always meant my mother had made the rounds. A grandfather clock marked the hall in calm, unbothered intervals.

Family portraits lined the corridor leading to the dining room—Sinclairs in sepia and silver, shoulders squared, gowns immaculate, expressions carved from stone. None of them smiled. At the end of the hall, my father's oil portrait glared down from the early nineties: younger then, harder around the eyes, already carrying the weight of the name.

I passed them all and pushed through the double doors.

The chandelier spilled a warm wash over polished walnut and crystal. The table was staged the way Mom believed all tables should be—fresh flowers, linen napkins, the good silver that gleamed like proof of legacy. At one end, my father sat with a glass of red, posture as precise as ever, a man who could still the air in a room without raising his voice. At the other, my mother presided in silk and diamonds, poised so perfectly that even society wives lowered their tones when she entered a room.

She brightened when she saw me, reaching with both hands as I bent to kiss her cheek. "You're working yourself too thin, Ezra," she murmured, warmth threaded with command. "I can see it on your face. Sit down before your father drinks the good bottle without you."

"Your mother underestimates me," my father said, without looking up from his glass.

Her presence loosened something tight in my chest, if only for a breath. I slid into my usual seat halfway down, the one I'd occupied since I was old enough to talk back.

Julian was already sprawled beside me, tie half-undone, hair damp from a shower that had been an afterthought. He smirked. "Look who finally showed. We were about to start without you."

"Don't tempt me," Mom said lightly, not sparing him a glance. And like always, he straightened at the sound of her voice. Every son did.

Footsteps and silver. A server appeared with lamb and roasted potatoes, another with greens glossed in butter. Across the table, Vivienne sat in perfect posture, polished as ever, but her eyes darted to me and Julian with a flicker that betrayed her—an old habit from the years when the three of us were inseparable. When we weren't opponents. Her mouth tightened, though she smoothed it quickly, her husband's hand already draped across her chair like a claim.

"Ezra," my father said, "Vivienne was just telling us Malcolm will accompany her to the Clairborne gala next week."

I set my napkin down carefully. "Funny. I thought I was attending on behalf of Sinclair Holdings."

Vivienne's chin lifted, her tone calm but measured. "It isn't about who attends. It's about showing steadiness."

Mom cut into her lamb, voice soft as velvet, sharp as glass. "Steadiness is a fine thing, sweetheart. But only if people are clear on who's guiding the ship. Otherwise, they might start thinking anyone with a hand on the wheel has a claim to steer it."

She didn't look up when she said it. She didn't have to.

Malcolm gave a low chuckle, though his smile thinned at the edges. "Of course. But family works best when everyone pulls together."

Mom dabbed delicately at her mouth. "Mmm. True enough. But some ties are stronger than others. That's what keeps us from drifting."

Vivienne shifted, eyes flicking between me and Julian before settling on her plate. That old look again—the one that said she hated being forced to choose sides.

Julian leaned back, whistling low. "Well. Note to self—never test Mama's metaphors."

Laughter rippled across the table, but the line had already been drawn.

I lifted my glass, staring into the dark swirl of red. Vivienne hadn't spoken against me, but she hadn't stood with me either. And I couldn't blame her. She was caught—between the husband she'd chosen and the brothers she'd once stood shoulder-to-shoulder with.

Once, the three of us had been a team. Now we were pieces on opposite ends of the board.

The hum of silverware filled the silence, but all I could hear was Noelle's laugh—bright, reckless. And all I could see was the way she'd looked at me before another man's name had dropped into the room like a stone.

My grip tightened on the stem of my glass, swallowing hard against the weight of both tables—the one I sat at now, and the one I couldn't get out of my head.

***

Dinner dissolved the way it always did—my father retreating to his study without a word, Vivienne and Malcolm slipping off in quiet unison, Julian vanishing with a grin and mischief in his eyes.

I pushed back my chair, ready to escape to my own house, when my mother's voice called me back.
"Walk with me, sweetheart."

Her hand brushed mine as we moved down the corridor into her sitting room. Softer than the rest of the house, it carried her imprint: walls lined with photographs instead of portraits, books stacked in even towers, the faint sweetness of magnolia from the candle she always kept burning.

She lowered herself onto the couch, smoothing her skirt, and patted the space beside her. I loosened my tie before sitting.

For a long moment, she studied me. Those eyes—warm, sharp, unyielding—could always see past the surface.
"You've been carrying the company on your back since your father stepped down. I see it. And I see what it's cost you. That's why I asked you to try this matchmaking business." Her voice softened, but her gaze didn't waver. "Tell me. How's it been going since we last spoke?"

I rubbed my jaw. "The first was a disaster. The second… better. But not enough."

Her brows lifted, hope flickering. "Better's still a beginning."

"Not when I have to stay stuck with whomever I pick for the long run," I muttered.

She reached across and covered my hand with hers. Her rings were cool against my skin, her grip deceptively gentle. "That's exactly why this matters. Numbers don't keep you in that chair. Appearances do. Stability does. People need to see you with someone who looks like forever, even if it takes time for it to feel that way."

My shoulders stiffened, but she pressed on,
"You can grow into love, Ezra. Your father and I—don't think it was effortless. We learned each other. But we looked right together from the start. That was half the battle won."

I turned toward the window, jaw tight. Looked right. The words sat heavier than they should have.

Her thumb brushed once against my knuckles, a small, almost tender gesture that didn't blunt the edge of her meaning. "Don't let pride cost you the company your granddaddy built. Find someone who steadies you in their eyes, even if your heart lags behind."

The message was clear: brilliance in the boardroom meant nothing without the right silhouette beside me.

I nodded once, face unreadable. "Yes, ma'am."

Her smile bloomed faint, satisfied, as if the matter were settled. But when she withdrew her hand, the echo of her words lingered louder than her voice.

Look right. Stability. Appearances.

And all I could think about was Noelle Collins—curls undone, laughter reckless, utterly uncurated. The opposite of what appearances demanded. And yet the only thing that had truly held me in years.

I couldn't face the silence of my house, not with her laugh still alive in my head. I needed air. Noise. Something strong enough to burn it out.

So I drove. Past the gates. Past the manicured hedges and the old weight of the Sinclair name until the city swallowed me again.

Ten minutes later, I slid into my spot at the lounge. My hideaway. The lights low, the jazz live, the air heavy with smoke and anonymity. A bar where no one asked questions they didn't want answers to.

The bartender caught my eye and poured without a word. I wrapped my hand around the glass, let the first burn of whiskey scrape the edge off my thoughts.

Here, I wasn't Ezra Sinclair, heir to Sinclair Holdings. Not the son my father measured, the brother my family circled, the man the board dissected.

Here, I was just a man trying not to drown in the quiet.

CHAPTER 16

Check by Proxy

Vivienne

Vivienne slipped into the quiet of her home, the symmetry of brick and white columns glowing under the lanterns. Inside, roses lingered faintly in the air—a housekeeper's touch she'd long since stopped noticing, except tonight. Malcolm kissed her temple, murmured something about follow-ups, and disappeared into his study.

She was halfway up the stairs when his voice carried through the cracked door.

"…I've already spoken with Pierce and Davenport. They see it the way I do—Ezra's marital status is a liability. A man with no wife, no children? It's instability waiting to happen. The board won't back a dynasty that ends with one man."

Vivienne froze, fingers tightening around the banister.

Malcolm's tone deepened, calculating, "Yeah, I planted the seed. Framed it as business, not personal. Perception matters more than ability in this world. Stability is marriage. Continuity is heirs. Ezra refuses to see that. And until he does, he'll always look temporary."

Silence. Then the faint clink of glass against wood.

"With Vivienne, I give them the opposite. A partnership that projects permanence. Alliances, the promise of children to carry the name forward. That's what anchors an empire. Some of them are starting to say it aloud now—what they only whispered before: Ezra may run the numbers, but he doesn't ground the family. We do."

Her throat went tight. He wasn't just praising her. He was wielding her—proof that he belonged in Ezra's place.

Malcolm's voice dropped lower, sharper, like a blade hidden under velvet. "Let's keep an eye on him. Every move. Every meeting. The board's patience has limits. The more I remind them of what he lacks, the easier it becomes to convince them he isn't the future. We are."

Vivienne's chest ached. He was setting her brother up for a fall, and he was doing it with her name on his lips.

She slipped down the hall before he could catch her listening, retreating into the bedroom. A drawer creaked open beneath her hand. Beneath brittle notes and gala programs lay a photograph: three children at their grandfather's community center ribbon-cutting. Ezra, tall even then, jaw already set with responsibility. Julian, grinning wide, tugging them both close. And herself in the middle, hands linked like a bridge.

Back then, it had been simple. No board politics. No marriage stakes. Just siblings.

Her thumb lingered over Ezra's face. She hated picturing him carrying the empire alone while her husband plotted to frame his life as a failure.

The photo blurred. She blinked hard, slid it back into the drawer, and closed it with care.

Downstairs, Malcolm's voice still carried—smooth, persuasive, relentless.

Vivienne straightened, the ache in her chest sharpening into something harder. To the world, she was half of a perfect couple. But in this quiet, she knew the truth: one day, she would have to choose.

CHAPTER 17

Velvet Cages

Noelle

I stood in front of the mirror longer than I meant to, smoothing the skirt of my dress, twirling the same curl around my finger, second-guessing the earrings I'd already decided on twice. It wasn't nerves, not really. I knew Greg. I'd known him too well, once. But somewhere in the space between his text and my "yes," hope had crept back in—small, inconvenient, insistent.

Hope that maybe the years had sharpened him, that he'd finally learned the kind of love I'd spent my life helping other people find. Foolish, maybe. But still.

The dress I'd chosen was soft cream, elegant without being a statement. I told myself I wanted to look effortless. Truth was, I didn't want to look like I'd tried too hard. A swipe of gloss, a touch of perfume, nothing more.

As I fastened the last clasp, my mind flickered—unbidden—back to Ezra. His hand braced steady against the jack, sleeves rolled, grease streaking the cuffs of a shirt that probably cost more than my rent when I first opened Collins & Co. The fact that a man with every resource at his disposal—a driver, staff only a phone call away—chose instead to crouch on hot asphalt and change my tire himself… it went beyond courtesy. For someone like him, it was a kind of intimacy. A selfless act that stripped away the armor of wealth and status. And for me, it was disarming to be cared for instead of always being the one who had to figure it out.

It wasn't romantic. It wasn't supposed to be anything. But I'd seen him differently in that moment. Not just as another powerful man defined by pride, but as someone who, in his own unguarded way, knew how to take care of others.

I shook the thought off quickly. Ezra Sinclair was not my story. Not even close. Tonight was about Greg. About seeing if there was anything worth salvaging.

A horn sounded out front, sharp and familiar. I slipped into my heels, grabbed my clutch, and squared my shoulders.

By the time I opened the door, Greg was already stepping out of his car. Same smile, same smoothness, dressed sharp in a suit he probably thought said something about how well he was doing. For a second, I let myself remember the charm—the way it hadn't been hard to fall for once.

"Noelle," he said, voice warm as he looked me over. "You look incredible."

I smiled, polite, even as my stomach knotted with something I couldn't quite name. Nerves, maybe a thread of apprehension.

"Ready?"

I nodded, letting him open the door for me. My reflection caught in the window as I slid inside, my expression already betraying the truth I wasn't ready to admit:

I wasn't sure if I wanted this dinner to prove me right… or wrong.

***

The lounge was warm and dim, the kind of place that wanted you to forget clocks existed. Candlelight flickered against gold-framed mirrors, the saxophone low and sweet in the corner. Greg held the door, hand at my back like old times, his cologne startling in its familiarity.

"You look incredible, Noelle." His voice carried that soft, almost boyish sincerity I hadn't expected. "I can't believe I ever let you go."

I smiled, the kind that kept distance. "Well, here we are."

The hostess led us to a booth, velvet cushions sinking me back into memory. Greg ordered the wine without asking—like he used to. I let him. The first sip was smooth, warm, and for a second, I almost forgot the habit behind the gesture.

We talked. His cases, the hours that kept him chained to late nights. My clients, the cities I'd expanded into. He listened, nodding, smiling like the years hadn't sharpened our edges. It felt almost too familiar, like falling back into a dance I hadn't forgotten.

"Collins & Co.," he said at last, leaning in, elbows braced. "I've been following. You've built something powerful." He tilted closer, voice low. "Honestly? I'm proud of you."

Warmth flared in my chest before I could stop it.

Then he tilted his head, smiling the same smile that had once disarmed me. "I just… never imagined you'd still be grinding this hard. I always thought, one day, you'd slow down. Family. Travel. More balance. Not twenty-four-seven clients." His laugh was soft, but it caught in my chest like a splinter.

The warmth cooled as quickly as it had come.
I set my glass down. "Balance doesn't mean giving up what I love."

"Of course," he said quickly, palms open. "Of course. I just mean—you deserve a soft life."

It sounded harmless, but it wasn't new. It was the echo of a man who once measured love by how much I would be willing to give up for him, while he never thought to give up anything for me.

The food came. We talked around it—holidays, my family, a story that made him laugh. He reached across the table, brushing my fingers like muscle memory.

And then: "I miss this. I miss you."

The saxophone slid into a note aching in the background. My chest tightened—not with longing, but recognition.

"You miss the version of me that made you most comfortable."

His expression faltered, then hardened. The charm slipped, sharpness flashing through.

"All you had to do," he said, voice low but cutting, "was play your role. Be the dutiful future wife. Instead, you buried yourself in clients and late nights, left me alone, neglected me—and I'm the villain for filling the void? Tell me, Noelle, is it really my fault in the end?"

It felt like a slap, the old wound tearing open again. I didn't need to imagine it—I remembered. The messages I'd found. Her name, her words, his replies threaded through with the same promises he made to me. The nights I tried to forgive, to patch over betrayal with the hope that he'd choose us again. And still, even when I gave him another chance, he kept seeing her.

He leaned back, tone smoothing again, manipulative and coaxing. "I was willing to give you anything. The world. Still am. But you never wanted it the way I offered it."

The ache in my body sharpened into clarity. I leaned back, appetite gone. "What we had was real, Greg. But real doesn't always mean right."

His eyes—regretful, maybe even loving—should've shaken me. Instead, they settled me. Because now I saw it plain: he hadn't broken me because I wasn't enough. He'd broken me because he needed less.

And I was never going to be less.

The quartet in the corner had shifted to In a Sentimental Mood, the sax player carried Coltrane's winding melancholy through the room. The notes curled low and heavy, fitting. Because no matter how much I tried to sit still and smile, the song matched my truth better than his words ever could.

I had been present. Always present. And it hadn't been enough.

My smile wavered. "Excuse me," I said softly, setting my napkin aside. "I need to use the restroom."

In the mirror, the truth stared back at me. Lipstick still perfect, curls still in place, dress exactly as I'd chosen—but beneath it, the faint crack in my composure.

What would I tell myself if I were my own client?

That if I don't honor what God placed in me—this vision, this fire—He'll pass it to someone bold enough to carry it. I'd tell her she deserves more than being minimized, and love— real love—doesn't punish you for standing in your own light. Most of all, I'd tell her a cage doesn't become a home just because someone lines it with velvet, and I wasn't built for cages.

For the first time all evening, I believed it.

I pulled my clutch from under the counter, phone already in hand. The rideshare app blinked up at me, reliable and merciful. I requested a car before I even thought twice.

The hostess gave me a warm smile as I passed, but Greg didn't notice me slip by. He was still seated at our table, phone angled in his hand, attention elsewhere—exactly as he'd been years ago when I realized what we had was never going to last.

Outside, the Houston night wrapped thick and humid around me. The neon from the lounge's sign painted the sidewalk in a glow of pink and gold. I stepped closer to the curb, the buzz of passing cars rising as I checked the screen. Five minutes until my driver arrived.

For the first time all night, I let myself breathe.
And then, as if summoned by the very air, I felt it—that shift, that steadying presence.

I looked up.
Ezra Sinclair stood near the valet line, tall against the glow of the city, his gaze pinned to me with quiet, unnerving focus.

The city moved around us—valet calls, horns, laughter spilling from the lounge—but it all dulled under the gravity of him standing there staring at me, as if the universe had drawn a line straight between us.

The ride couldn't come fast enough. But a part of me already knew—leaving one man behind might mean walking straight into a storm.

CHAPTER 18

Coltrane and Confessions

Ezra

This bar was my place. I came here when I wanted quiet dressed up as company—dim lights, Coltrane bleeding low through the speakers, whiskey poured without me asking.

And then she walked in.

Noelle.

A roomful of women could be in here, and I still would've only seen her. Cream dress. Curls catching the soft gold glow of the sconces, the kind of presence that made even a quiet booth feel like a stage. Beautiful didn't begin to cover it. She carried herself like she belonged everywhere, and somehow, like nowhere had ever been quite enough for her.

I should've looked away. Should've let her evening be her own. But then I saw him. The man she was with—suit crisp, smile a little too cocky, hand settling at her back like she was—his.

Just the thought had me ready to go over there.

At first, she played the part. Polite smiles. Measured nods. But I noticed what he didn't—the way her fingers tightened around her glass, how her smile thinned when he leaned too close, the shadow in her eyes that had nothing to do with nerves. It was unease. Sadness, even. Nothing like the woman I knew.

And that was the thing: I'd seen her in too many versions not to notice the contrast. The businesswoman. The matchmaker. The joy on her face on the pickleball courts, the fire alive in her eyes. That was Noelle Collins—vivid, uncontainable.

But here, with him? She looked dimmed. Pulled in.

Every instinct said to get up, cross the room, take her out of that booth and away from him. The urge was sharp, territorial. Jealousy, plain and unvarnished. I didn't even know the man, but I hated the way he looked at her—the entitlement, and worse, like he didn't give a damn about how she felt.

I got up to end the charade, but she moved.

Napkin folded with precision, her chin lifted high like armor. She slid from the booth, heels clicking across the floor with the kind of grace that left no cracks to anyone else's eye. But I knew what I'd seen.

The man barely looked up, his attention glued to his phone, thumb scrolling, while the best thing in the room slipped away unnoticed.

Minutes dragged, slow and heavy. My glass stayed full. My pulse didn't.

And then I saw her. The doors pushed open, and she stepped out into the night—clutch in hand, shoulders straight but trembling at the edges. The kind of composure you wear when you're about to crack.

I was already approaching her.

Neon light from the lounge's sign bled pink and gold across her skin, wrapping her in something too soft for the look on her face. Her clutch was tight in her hand, shoulders squared like she was bracing against the world. And then—I saw it. The shine at the corner of her eyes, catching the glow before she wiped it away.

Tears.

That was it.

Noelle Collins, who could dismantle a man's ego with just a few words, who laughed without apology, who built a multimillion dollar business from the ground up—crying in the street over a man who couldn't even put his phone down?

No.

She was too powerful for that. Too rare. Too her.

And yet as I closed the distance, heat burning steady under my skin, one thought cut through all the rest:

Why the hell did this matter so much to me?

Why did I want to tear whatever hurt her apart, and be the one who fixed it?

I closed in the space between us.

Her hand darted to her cheek the second she saw me, swiping away the trace of tears like they'd never been there. Chin lifted. Mask back on.

"Ezra," she said evenly, though her voice wavered at the edges. "What are you doing out here?"

"Making sure you're all right." My tone was low, warm. I didn't look away from her eyes.

She gave a quick, practiced smile. "I'm fine."

"You don't look fine."

"I said I'm fine." She gripped her clutch tighter, as if she could will it to anchor her.

I studied her for a long time, then asked, "Do you want to go home?"

Her breath hitched, and for a second I thought she might say yes. But then she shook her head, sharp, defiant. "No."

Something in me loosened. If she wasn't ready to retreat, then maybe—just maybe…

"Good," I said simply. "I know a place."

She glanced down, canceled the car, and nodded.

***

The drive was quiet, the city sliding past in streaks of neon and shadow. She sat beside me in the backseat, composed but not entirely at ease. My driver didn't ask questions—he never did. Ten minutes later, we were pulling up to one of my downtown offices, the steel and glass faintly glowing against the night.

Inside, the lobby lights were dim, the elevators empty. I swiped us to the top floor, then led her through the silent corridors until we reached the access door. One push and we were out under the open sky.

The rooftop stretched wide, ringed with low railings and the hum of the city below. Houston spread out in every direction—headlights tracing the highways, buildings rising like quiet sentinels. The air was cooler here, easier to breathe.

"This is one of my favorite places," I said, stepping to the ledge. "When I need quiet, or when I need to remember the city doesn't own me."

She joined me, arms folded, curls tugged by the breeze. For once, she didn't have a ready reply.

I ducked back inside the stairwell, returned with a bottle from my office stash—whiskey, smooth and sharp. I twisted the cap, poured into two paper cups I'd found, and handed her one.

"To not wanting to go home," I said.

Her lips curved faintly as she tapped her cup to mine. "To not wanting to go home."

The whiskey burned warm down my throat, cutting the edge off the night. For a moment we just stood there, side by side, the city humming below us.

Then I spoke. Quiet. Honest. "When I am up here I spend my life trying to be what everyone else expects. The son. The

CEO. The one who always has everything together. But it never feels like enough. No matter how many deals I close, no matter how much value I deliver… there's always another measure. Another test. And I wonder sometimes if I even exist outside of all that."

She turned, eyes softening. "Ezra…"

I shook my head, cutting her off before pity could slip through. "I'm not telling you this for sympathy. I just… figured if I went first, maybe it'd make it easier for you to tell me what had you walking out of that dinner like you couldn't breathe."

Her fingers tightened around the cup. For a long moment she didn't speak, gaze fixed on the lights below. Then—

"He broke my heart once." Her voice was steady, but low. "The man you saw me with. Years ago, I thought he was it. My forever. But he never wanted the woman I actually am. And when I didn't comply with his requests… he found someone who did. I told myself I was past it. That I could face him again. But sitting across from him tonight, hearing the same callous words dressed up as something new… it hit me harder than I expected."

She laughed, humorless. "Pathetic, right?"

"No." My answer came sharper than I meant. I caught her gaze, held it. "It's not pathetic to want to believe people can change. It's human. The pathetic part is when a man has a woman like you and still can't appreciate her."

Her eyes widened slightly, breath catching. She looked away first, but not before I saw it—the flicker of heat, of knowing.

The silence stretched again, but softer this time. Less like a weight, more like a thread pulling taut between us.

She tipped her cup back, draining it, then let out a slow breath. "You shouldn't be telling me things like that."

"Why?"

"Because I might start believing you're not who I thought you were and I'm rarely wrong."

I let the corner of my mouth curve. "Maybe I'm not."

The city hummed on below us, endless and alive. She shifted closer without realizing it, shoulder brushing mine. I didn't move away. Didn't want to.

And standing there, alcohol warm in my veins and her presence anchoring me in a way I hadn't expected, I knew the truth settling in my chest like something I couldn't fight—

I was falling for her.

Her words lingered between us, carried off by the wind, but her eyes stayed fixed on the skyline. A curl had slipped loose, brushing against her cheek in the breeze.

Before I could stop myself, I reached up. My fingers brushed it back, slow, deliberate, tucking it behind her ear. My hand hovered there a beat too long, close enough to feel the heat of her skin, close enough to see her pupils widen just slightly.

She froze. Her breath caught.

I should've stepped back. Instead, I leaned in, drawn by something I couldn't name. Her eyes flicked up to mine, and for a heartbeat, there was nothing else. Just the pull. Just the question of what would happen if I closed the distance.

Her lips parted. Mine nearly followed.

And then—she turned. Just enough. A sharp breath, a shift back toward the skyline. "We shouldn't," she murmured.

The space snapped back between us like a rubber band.

I cleared my throat, forcing composure. "Right. We shouldn't."

But the truth? I wanted to. Badly.

***

The whiskey kept flowing, loosening the edges that had felt so sharp before. She shifted the conversation, quick and purposeful, latching onto lighter topics—our worst first dates, bad travel stories, the most ridiculous client requests she'd received. I followed her lead, offering pieces of myself I didn't usually share: the time Julian almost set fire to the garage trying to brew beer, the one fight Vivienne had ever won against me as a kid.

Her laugh came unrestrained now, and every time it did, I caught myself staring. She looked different when she was happy—beautiful in a way that had nothing to do with the dress or the skyline. And I knew I wanted to be the reason she stayed that way.

"You're enjoying this too much," she accused, shaking her head, eyes sparkling.

"I'm enjoying watching you relax," I countered, pouring us both another round. "And making you laugh."

Her eyes narrowed, but the smile tugging at her mouth betrayed her. "Don't get ahead of yourself, Sinclair. You almost sound charming."

"Hard to believe, huh?" I said, clinking my cup to hers.

She rolled her eyes at me with a smile, softening her posture. At some point, she drew her knees up to her chest, resting her chin there like she'd done it a thousand times before. The city noise faded, leaving just the low thrum of traffic, the occasional gust of wind, her presence beside me.

She yawned, covering it with the back of her hand, then leaned sideways almost absently. Her head landed against my shoulder.

I went rigid for half a second, every instinct screaming not to move, not to ruin the fragile peace of it. Then I exhaled slow, shifted just enough to make it comfortable.

Her breathing evened, her weight warm against me. One hand slipped to her lap, fingers curled loosely around the empty paper cup.

I stared out over the skyline, but my thoughts weren't on the city. They were on her. On the laugh that had disarmed me, the fire that had challenged me, the quiet that had undone me tonight.

And for the first time in years, I didn't feel restless on this rooftop. I didn't feel trapped by the name Sinclair.

I just felt… happy.

CHAPTER 19

The Art of Appearances

Noelle

A hand brushed my arm.

"Noelle."

My eyes blinked open to a pale gray sky bleeding into dawn. Disoriented, I shifted, then froze as I realized my cheek had been pressed against Ezra's shoulder. His jacket was draped over me, heavy and warm, carrying his scent.

He was still there. Staring at the sunrise with that unreadable intensity.

"Morning," he said quietly.

Heat rushed up my neck. I sat up straighter, clutching at the lapels, smoothing my hair with one hand, wishing I didn't care how I looked, but suddenly caring too much. "God. I—did I fall asleep?"

"Looks that way." His turned his gaze to me, smiling faintly. "You snore, by the way."

I shot him a look, half-mortified, until I caught the gleam in his eyes. Teasing. I almost laughed despite myself. Almost.

"I should go," I murmured, reaching for my clutch.

"I'll take you." He rose easily, offering his hand. I hesitated, then let him pull me up. His grip was warm, steady— too steady for how unsteady I suddenly felt.

Down on the street, his driver was already waiting. Ezra opened the door, and I hesitated again, still wrapped in his jacket, aware of how rumpled I must look and how much I didn't want to give it back.

"Thank you," I said at last.

His gaze caught mine, something quiet and unresolved flickering there. "Anytime."

I slipped into the car, tugging the jacket closer. As the door shut and the city blurred past the window, I let out a breath I hadn't realized I'd been holding. His scent clung to me the whole ride home, making me feel both comforted and exposed.

***

By the time Shayla rang the bell, the late morning sun was already spilling through my kitchen windows, catching on the champagne flutes I'd set out for our emergency brunch

She breezed in, balancing a pastry box in one hand and champagne in the other. "We're doing mimosas," she said, no preamble. "Coffee's not strong enough for what you texted me last night."

I couldn't help laughing as I hugged her. "You didn't even ask what happened."

"Didn't need to." She popped the cork in one clean move, poured, and slid a glass toward me. "That *"Girl!"* said everything. Now—talk."

She perched on the stool across from me, her ring catching the light. My proudest match, sitting right here ready to mother me like only Shayla could.

I took a long sip before answering. "Dinner was… fine. On the surface. Greg was charming. He said all the right things, at first."

Her brows lifted knowingly. "At first?"

I exhaled. "The second I sat there, it was like no time had passed. I remembered everything—the way he made me feel like my work was somehow too much, like I was too much.

And worse… I remembered *that girl* "coming to me as a woman"."

Shayla's smile faded, her voice low. "The one from the department store."

I nodded, throat tight. "I told myself I could forgive it all. That time would dull it. But sitting across from him? Plus after some of what he said, I realized I'd never stop asking myself if it would happen again the moment I didn't fit the version of me he wanted. His lack of remorse made it clear to me it would."

For a moment, the only sound was the fizz of the champagne between us. Then Shayla reached across and squeezed my hand. "You're an incredible, powerful, multi-faceted woman. You don't get to forget that because some man couldn't handle the blessing he had. That's his failure, not yours."

My eyes stung. I blinked hard, managing a shaky laugh. "Why do you always sound like you should be the one running a matchmaking firm?"

"Because my matchmaker trained me well," she shot back with a grin, holding up her ring. "Best investment I ever made."

We laughed, clinked glasses, and tore into the croissants. For a little while, it felt like old times—two women, carbs, bubbles, and honesty.

But Shayla wasn't finished. She tilted her head, giving me that look that had cut through my excuses since college. "So. That's Greg. But why is a man's suit jacket laying across your couch?"

I twisted the stem of my glass, the bubbles catching in my throat before I finally exhaled. "There was… someone else last night. Not like that," I added quickly when her brows shot up. "But—Ezra Sinclair was there."

Shayla's brows flew up. She sat back, lips parting before she let out a low laugh.

"Wait. *Ezra Sinclair*? Mr. Billion-Dollar Bachelor himself?"

Heat crept up my neck. "Yeah. Him."

Shayla leaned in, eyes bright now. "Okay, no—run that back. You're telling me you had dinner with Greg *and* ran into Houston's favorite fantasy all in one night? I need details, all of them, now."

"I didn't expect him. Didn't plan to see him outside of the office. But we have been running into each other lately. When I came out of the restaurant, there he was—watching me like he could see past everything I was trying to hold together."

The words spilled easier than I meant them to. "We talked. Not about business—at least, not really. Just… about life, about how heavy it all feels sometimes. And for a moment, it was like neither of us was carrying our names or our jobs. Just two people on a rooftop, trying to breathe and be heard."

Shayla leaned forward, chin in her palm, eyes bright. "And how did that feel?"

I hesitated, pressing a hand to my glass like I could still the fizz. "Like something I shouldn't want. But also… like something I've been missing."

She didn't say anything right away, just reached across and touched my hand. And that silence—that knowing—was almost worse than words.

***

Sadie appeared in the doorway without knocking, tablet clutched like it was a top secret file.

"Noelle," she said, low but urgent. "You need to see this."

I barely looked up from the profile in front of me. "If it's another CEO's kid wanting a plus-one for Aspen, pass."

Her heels clicked sharp across the floor. She set the tablet down in front of me. Not words this time—an image.
Ezra Sinclair. Standing outside a lounge. Head bent low toward

a woman in cream, her curls half-shadowed, the angle blurred but recognizable in a way that made my pulse catch.

"Tell me this isn't you," Sadie whispered.

The headline scrolled beneath: *Houston's Most Eligible Bachelor Spotted with Mystery Woman. Is Sinclair Off the Market?*

The photo landed like a fist beneath my sternum, but my face stayed smooth. 'It's grainy. Could be anyone.'

Sadie's brow arched. "Except it isn't."

I exhaled once, slow. "How far has it spread?"

"Two blogs. One gossip account already reposted it. If you want my professional opinion? It'll be everywhere by dinner."

Not if I moved fast.

I reached for my phone, thumb flying to a contact list built over years of favors, quiet donations, and very expensive dinners. Within minutes I had three people working in tandem: one sending cease-and-desist letters, Andre reminding a certain blogger of the NDA they'd signed at a past gala, another seeding a distraction piece about a celebrity divorce. By the time I hung up, the article had vanished. Link dead. Post gone.

Sadie exhaled like she'd been holding her breath the entire time. "Sometimes I forget how scary you can be."

"Good," I said, smoothing the edge of the folder on my desk. "That means other people do too."

Her laugh was thin, but the admiration was there. "Still—" she hesitated, eyes flicking toward the tablet, "—if people saw it once, they'll remember. Screenshots don't erase."

She was right. The thought coiled hot in my gut, but I slid the tablet aside with practiced calm.

Control restored. At least, that's what I told myself.

The office settled into silence again. The view stretched wide from my floor-to-ceiling windows, Houston glittering against the late morning light. For a moment, I let myself pretend it was over.

Done.

That's exactly when I heard the softest knock—polite, deliberate. The kind of knock that announced itself without needing permission.

The door opened before Sadie could cross the room.

Evelyn Sinclair stepped inside like she'd been expected all along. Navy suit, pearl earrings, posture carved from marble. She carried the air of someone who had never been told no in her life—and wouldn't have accepted it if she had.

She gave Sadie a warm-enough smile that still dismissed her, then turned her attention fully on me.

"Noelle," she said smoothly. "I hope I'm not intruding."

"Of course not." I rose, every inch of me polished back into place. "What can I do for you, Mrs. Sinclair?"

She didn't sit right away. Instead, she traced a fingertip along the edge of the desk, pausing on the tablet Sadie had abandoned. Her eyes flicked up, calm but cutting. "I imagine you've already had a busy morning."

My throat tightened, but I kept my voice level. "If you're referring to the photo, it's been handled."

Her smile curved—polite, never warm. "Handled is a strong word. Erased, maybe. But you and I both know whispers last longer than pixels."

I folded my hands lightly on the desk. "Your son is my client. That's all there is to it."

"And I'm sure you mean that." She finally lowered herself into the chair across from me, her movements precise. "But intent isn't always what people see. People see what they want to. And when it comes to Ezra, perception is everything."

There it was—the velvet over steel.

She leaned in slightly, voice dropping. "My husband and I built a life on projecting stability, not just managing it. Ezra will need a partner who understands that. A woman whose family has weathered scrutiny before. Who knows how to hold a name steady under pressure." Her gaze sharpened, pinning me in place. "Someone who adds value to the legacy, not question marks."

The weight of her words landed heavy. I nodded once, steady. "Of course. That's my goal. To find him exactly that."

Evelyn sat back, smoothing her skirt, satisfied. "I knew we understood each other." She rose, the pearls at her throat catching the light. "Ezra's future depends on it. Our family's reputation depends on it"

Her heels clicked toward the door. Before she left, she glanced back with that poised, lethal smile.
"And so, perhaps, does yours."

The door shut behind her, soft as a whisper.

But the words didn't fade with her perfume. They stayed, coiled tight in my chest. Evelyn hadn't been making conversation—she'd been making a promise. My career, everything I'd built, hung on delivering Ezra a match. If I failed—or worse, if she decided I was the problem instead of the solution—she had the power to ruin me and my family. And I didn't doubt for a second that she would.

Sadie shifted in the doorway, quiet but watchful. "She doesn't play."

"No," I said softly, eyes on Ezra's file. "She doesn't."

And neither could I.

I set the tablet aside and pressed my pen harder than necessary against the page.

I wasn't here to be his storm.

I was here to find him his match.

CHAPTER 20

The Queen's Sacrifice

Noelle

The moment Evelyn left my office, I pulled Ezra's file toward me like it could anchor me back to center. Silver-embossed leather, heavier than paper had any right to be. Inside: profiles, notes, vetted matches that checked every box.

Boxes Evelyn would approve of.

I told myself this wasn't personal. That this was business, and business meant results. By the third date, I prided myself on knowing whether a match had staying power. Ezra Sinclair wasn't going to be the first client to slip through my hands. Not when eyes were already watching.

Still, my pen hovered too long over the page.

Tall, poised, legacy name. Another with a law degree from Columbia and a family foundation worth eight figures. Perfect on paper. Perfect for Evelyn. Perfect for the Sinclair legacy.

But I kept seeing him at the lounge, standing outside under the city lights, his gaze trained on me like the world had gone quiet. I kept hearing the softness in his voice when grease streaked his cuffs and he told me to let him help. The man in those moments didn't need a merger in heels. He needed something else.

And yet I knew—whatever he needed, it could never be me. Not really. Not once people dug deeper. Because if anyone ever peeled back the polished veneer I'd built, if they saw past the neat introductions and careful curation, they'd find my brother. His lifestyle. His record. A history the Sinclairs would never excuse, no matter how much they liked my smile or respected my business.

On top of that, my family wasn't old money. We weren't oil, shipping, or steel. We weren't the kind of wealthy that bought immunity. I had built something, yes—but not the kind of empire their world called legacy. And legacy was their language.

It was impractical. Unrealistic, even, to entertain the possibility of Ezra Sinclair looking at me the way I sometimes caught him looking. No matter how much I wanted to memorize the sound of his laugh, or the weight of his gaze when it stripped away every defense I had, I needed to stay focused.

Focused on results. On survival.

I flipped the file closed and slid a different profile to the top: a woman with a last name everyone knew, a family empire in oil and shipping. Accomplished, charming, the kind of woman Evelyn had described to me not even an hour ago.

"She's good," I murmured, making notes for the team. "The kind of good that holds under pressure."

Sadie knocked lightly, stepping in with her tablet. "You're locking him for date three?"

"Yes," I said without looking up. "Third date is decision territory. I won't fail him."

Her pause lingered. "You sound like you're trying to convince yourself."

I finally glanced up, my smile polished and immovable. "Sometimes conviction is a practice. That's what makes it stick."

She studied me for a second, then nodded, slipping out of the room.

Alone again, I let the mask slide for half a breath. My pen tapped against the edge of Ezra's folder, steady and betraying nothing.

Evelyn was right: perception mattered. Legacy mattered.

So why did it feel like the one thing I couldn't put in a folder… was the only thing that mattered to me?

***

I had the file open before he arrived, pages spread with practiced precision. Every bullet point was lined up like armor: background, assets, philanthropic interests. Alexandra Martin wasn't just a match. She was the kind of woman the world expected Ezra Sinclair to be with—charismatic, pedigreed, untouchable. Exactly what Evelyn would approve of.

When the door clicked shut behind him, the temperature seemed to shift. He filled the room easily, like he owned the air. charcoal suit, shoulders cut sharp, cufflinks glinting under the morning light—and that steady gaze that made me want to forget my own name.

"Morning," he said, voice low.

"Mr. Sinclair," I returned, formal, measured, as if my heartbeat wasn't already traitorous. "Please, have a seat."

He did, but he didn't lean back. He leaned forward, elbows on his knees, eyes fixed squarely on me while I spoke. It made the words sharper than I intended.

"I've confirmed your third date. Alexandra Martin. She's on the board of her family's shipping empire, sits on multiple philanthropic councils, and was listed on *Houston Business Journal*'s '40 Under 40.'" I slid the file toward him. "She is intelligent, influential, and understands the weight of legacy. I believe she represents the kind of partnership that would suit you—personally and publicly."

He didn't so much as glance at the folder. His eyes stayed locked on mine, unreadable. "That sounded less like a match," he said slowly, "and more like a press release."

I stiffened. "It's my job to consider more than attraction. Reputation matters. Stability matters."

His mouth curved, but it wasn't amusement—it was something sharper. "And what if I told you I don't give a damn about Alexandra Martin?"

My pulse tripped, but my tone stayed even. "Then you'd be wasting both of our time."

Silence stretched. The only sound was the faint tick of the Cartier clock on my desk, steady and merciless. Then he leaned in farther, his voice quieter, more dangerous.

"What if what I want is sitting right in front of me?"

The air left my chest. For a moment, the city vanished outside the glass, the whole building narrowing down to the space between his gaze and mine. His words weren't slick, weren't calculated. They carried weight, and it was terrifying.

I forced myself to move, to breathe, to lift my chin. "You are my client, Ezra. That's all."

Something flickered in his eyes—frustration, maybe hurt—but he didn't look away. "Funny. Because I don't feel like 'just a client' when you look at me like that."

Heat burned across my skin. "I don't—"

"Yes, you do." His voice cut soft, not cruel. "The rest of them see Sinclair Holdings. My father's heir. The headlines. But you—" His jaw tightened, like he regretted letting it slip. "You're different."

The weight of it nearly undid me, but I reached for steel instead. "I see you as a man who hired me to find him a match. And I will. Ms. Martin is an excellent choice. *The right choice.*"

He finally leaned back, but his gaze stayed tethered to mine, unrelenting. "Fine. I'll meet her. I'll play it your way. But don't lie to yourself, Noelle."

I gripped the Montblanc pen until my knuckles ached. "Lie to myself about what?"

His smile was faint, dangerous, the kind that said he already knew the answer. "About the fact that every time we're in the same room, neither of us is thinking about anyone else."

The words vibrated through the silence, daring me to break. I didn't. Couldn't. Though I wanted to….badly.

I forced the folder closer to him. "Date. Three. Alexandra Martin. That's the only thing you should be thinking about."

He finally leaned back, though the movement reluctant, like he was prying himself loose from something he didn't want to leave. For a long moment, he studied me, and I could see the question flicker across his face—the one he wouldn't say out loud. Had he misread everything?

At last, he picked up the folder, flipping it open with a quiet snap. "Fine. I'll give her a fair shot. A real one. Just so we're clear on where we stand."

The words weren't defiant this time. They were edged with something else. Something that almost sounded like doubt.

He rose smoothly, buttoning his jacket. His eyes lingered on me one last time, searching, waiting for something I wouldn't give.

When the door closed behind him, I was left with the echo of that look—and the ache of wondering if I'd built the distance so well that he might actually believe it.

CHAPTER 21
A Game with No Winners

Ezra

I walked into the restaurant braced for the kind of evening that felt like a business meeting with candles.

And then Alexandra Martin stood to greet me.

Black dress, diamonds catching the light, hair pinned back neat. But her smile—that surprised me. It was warm. Real. Carefree. It landed like she was actually glad to be there.

"Ezra," she said, offering her hand. "I'm glad we could finally meet. I was beginning to think Noelle brought you up just to justify her fee."

It disarmed me. A light tease. My mouth curved before I could stop it. "She's already got you running her playbook. That's new."

Her eyes glinted. "She warned me you'd be…a lot.

"And you believed her?"

"I told her I'm extra myself."

The line pulled a laugh out of me, low in my chest. Because it sounded like Noelle—calling me out without apology.

We sat. The city glowed outside the window, glass towers stacked against the night. Alexandra ordered Sancerre, raised a brow to see if I'd follow. I did. Then she carried the conversation—literacy programs she backed, shipping contracts she wrangled, a story about her nephews daring her onto a rollercoaster that had her laughing mid-sentence.

And for a while, it was good. Pleasant even.

She was smart. Confident without trying to sell me on it. She looked at me like a man across a table, not the CEO of a billion-dollar company. I almost forgot what this was supposed to be.

When the talk shifted to family business politics, her voice dipped. "It's all theater, isn't it? Half the time I feel like these people are auditioning for a role nobody actually wants."

Something tightened in me. That hint of cynicism, quiet but honest, was too close to someone else.

Noelle, frowning across her desk, telling me I treated her time like a game.

Noelle, reminding me I wasn't just my father's son.

Noelle, laughing like she'd forgotten the world could see her.

I blinked back to the woman in front of me. Alexandra smiled, calm and effortless, sipping her wine. She was—right. Or close enough to right that anyone else would call her perfect. Mom would adore her. The board would nod. The press would have their fairytale.

But as she spoke, as her laugh slipped into the low hum of the room, the comparison clawed in.

She was good. But she wasn't Noelle.

Dinner ended clean. No stumbles, no wrong notes. Her driver opened her door, she gave me a parting smile, and the car disappeared into the blur of city lights.

It had been everything it needed to be. Smooth. Promising. Alexandra Martin was the kind of choice that made sense.

But walking back to my car, the truth pressed heavy in my chest.

Sense wasn't the same as fire.

And the only woman who made me forget the weight of my own name—the only one who made me think beyond obligation—was the one who'd made it clear I could never have her.

The leather was cool against my shoulders as I slid into the back seat. Houston smeared past the window, neon bleeding into headlights until the city looked half-real. Alexandra's laugh lingered in my ears, sweet enough that I almost let myself believe it could be enough.

Almost.

I pulled out my phone. The screen glowed blue against my face, thumb hovering. The words formed slow, deliberate:

I think you found my match.

I stared at it long enough to feel the weight of every letter. Then I hit send.

The message disappeared, but the heaviness in my chest didn't move.

Because I knew—even as the city blurred past, even as Alexandra's smile replayed in my mind—that what I'd given Noelle wasn't the truth.

It was the move I was supposed to make in a game I couldn't win.

And the truth sat sharp, unspoken, lodged where I couldn't shake it: the only match that mattered was the one behind glass doors who was acting like she didn't want me.

PART III

SALT AND FIRE

CHAPTER 22

The Price of Preservation

Noelle—A month later

There was no avoiding them.

Ezra Sinclair and Alexandra Martin filled my feeds— blogs, radio chatter, trending hashtags.

On Instagram a gala photo kept resurfacing: Alexandra in a dress that threw light, Ezra at her side in a tux, his hand resting at her back. On TikTok their entrance played on loop, strangers narrating the arrival like they'd been invited to the table. Even the business pages framed it as "strategic alignment"—treating the relationship like a merger.

Together, they read inevitable. Powerful.

I did what I could. Mute. Block. Filter. I scrubbed searches until his name went quiet. For a little while, it worked.

Then the courier came.

He set it on my desk and was gone before I could respond. Black cardstock, edges foiled in gold, my name inked in calligraphy that seemed to already know too much. I slid a finger under the seal. The flap tore with a muted rip. Inside, on heavy cream paper, the words danced in elegant script: *The Sinclair family requests the honor of your presence for dinner at the Sinclair estate. Tomorrow evening.* Signed, Evelyn Sinclair.

Not an invitation. A summons.

I closed my eyes, but the words didn't go away.

Instead I was tugged back to the memory of his face in my office a month earlier, to the file on my desk smoothed flat, to the way the room had tightened when he walked in. He hadn't glanced at the dossier. He'd only looked at me.

"You're certain this is what's best?" he'd asked, voice low enough to be private and loud enough to own the space.

I lied. "Yes," I said. "She's the right match." He buttoned his jacket and left me with the echo of that look. "Goodbye, Ms. Collins."

Now Alexandra's smile glittered under chandeliers and Ezra's gaze angled toward her like she was gravity. That smile—the same one he gave me when I challenged him—belonged to me.

My chest constricted until I couldn't breathe easily. I looked up and Sadie's reflection hovered in the glass before she spoke.

"You okay?"

The answer ripped out of me. "I'm not." My hand went into a fist and dropped. "Clear my afternoon, Sadie." The first time I had ever said those words.

She nodded once and closed the door softly.

When I was alone the dam broke. I pressed my palm hard over my eyes, but the tears came anyway—hot, fast, merciless. One slid down and streaked the tablet screen, distorting Ezra's face and bending Alexandra's perfect smile into something ugly and human. Panic flared and I shoved the invitation and tablet into the drawer as if the drawer could swallow the world's story.

Hiding it didn't help. The truth had already taken root.

I hadn't just matched Ezra Sinclair. I'd smoothed his narrative into something that left no room for whatever we'd had. And Evelyn—if I had failed and she chose to pull at a single loose thread—she wouldn't have stopped until she unraveled everything.

A whisper escaped, small and raw. "What have I done to myself?"

***

The next morning, my feeds were quiet. No headlines bled across my screen. No photos waited in ambush when I opened a tab.

The silence of it all was almost worse. My phone, usually buzzing with alerts, felt heavy in my hand. The clean desktop, the cleared notifications—it was too sterile, like a room sealed off after something had died inside it.

My desk looked restored: files squared, pens aligned, order reestablished. Still, the relief was fragile, a thin veneer stretched over something jagged.

Mr. Callahan arrived early, as he always did, shaking me out of my thoughts. He carried himself differently this time— lighter, as if some invisible stone had shifted from his chest. His suit wasn't new, but it sat better on him, shoulders no longer sagging under the weight of memories. And then I saw it: his wedding band, no longer on his hand but strung on a chain around his neck. It caught the morning light when he sat down, gleaming against his shirt like a quiet confession.

"I thought it was time for an update," he said, settling into the chair across from me. His voice was still rough in places, but steadier than before.

I braced myself for a polite dismissal, the kind of report people give when they don't want to disappoint. Instead, his mouth curved into something softer.

"She's… wonderful," he said simply. "We've seen each other a few times now. She's not Margaret. She'll never be Margaret. But she's kind. Thoughtful. Easy to laugh with. Dinner didn't feel like a performance—it just felt… good."

Something in me eased at that word. *Good.* After months of watching him speak like every breath was rationed, hearing him say good was almost startling.

"I'm glad," I said, keeping my voice even though my throat caught. "That's exactly what I hoped for you."

He nodded, fingers brushing the chain at his collar. "Margaret was my once-in-a-lifetime," he said, steady, not mournful. "I'll never have that again. But I realized—I don't need to. I was lucky enough to have it once. Not everyone gets that. Everyone should, though. At least once."

The words landed heavier than he could know. I forced myself to hold his gaze, to smile the way a matchmaker should—warm, approving, composed. But his truth pierced me in a place I didn't want touched. Because he was right. There *was* such a thing as once-in-a-lifetime love. He'd lived it. He could open himself to something steady now because he'd already known the fire.

I'd built my reputation on steering people into futures they couldn't imagine for themselves. Even Ezra, with all his walls, had let me chart his course. But somewhere along the way, I had crossed my own line. One I vowed to avoid.

"I'm glad you've found someone who gives you peace," I said. And I meant it.

When Mr. Callahan left, my pen hovered above the page, but nothing came. Not a note, not a strategy. Just the sting behind my eyes, hot enough to blur the ink until the letters swam. My hand shook once, then I shoved the papers aside before I smeared them too.

His words clung, circling. *Everyone should experience it once.*

I had spent years convincing myself I was exempt. That logic and control were enough. That matches could be plotted like constellations—arranged until they formed something resembling permanence.

But in the silence of my office, with only the steady tick of the clock to answer me, the truth pressed in sharp and merciless.

What if I had already found it—and let it walk away?

***

The invitation sat on my vanity like it had been waiting for me all along. I'd turned it over a dozen times, half-hoping the letters might blur if I stared long enough. They never did.

I told myself I had no reason to go. Matchmakers weren't supposed to step into their clients' private lives. But this wasn't optional. Evelyn Sinclair didn't extend invitations; she issued a command. And tomorrow had become tonight.

The gown Sadie once bullied me into buying hung heavy against my skin—midnight silk, clean at the shoulder, the kind of dress that carried its own gravity. My reflection looked composed enough, but tension coiled under my ribs. I steadied myself with a swipe of red lipstick, armor disguised as paint, and slipped the tube into my clutch.

The driver arrived on time, black car idling as though it belonged outside my building. I gathered my clutch, forced my breath even, and slid into the back seat.

The city gave way from suburbs to sprawling land. The closer we came, the quieter it grew—until the only sound was the hum of tires on winding pavement. The estate unfolded in pieces: wrought-iron gates, lanterns burning like sentries, mansions scattered across the grounds, each one a kingdom.

I wondered which belonged to Ezra. My eyes caught on one—dark limestone, sharp against the sky, lit in a way that felt almost brooding. It fit. My stomach twisted.

I reminded myself: he was with Alexandra now. For all I knew, she would be at that table too. And if she was, I'd have no screen to close, no blog to mute, no post to scroll past. Just reality—Ezra Sinclair beside someone else. The thought pressed hard against my lungs.

The car slowed at the base of wide steps that climbed toward arched double doors. The driver opened my door with a quiet, "Ms. Collins."

The night air was cool, fragrant with manicured gardens I didn't stop to admire. My heels clicked softly against the stone as I ascended, each step measured though my pulse raced.

At the doors, I paused. The estate loomed around me, beautiful and imposing, built to remind anyone who approached that the Sinclairs weren't just wealthy—their legacy was carved in stone.

I tightened my grip on the clutch. One last breath. Then I lifted my hand and knocked.

The door opened quickly. A butler—impeccable in black, white gloves, expression unreadable—bowed as though I'd been expected all along.

"Ms. Collins," he said, not a question. "This way."

The foyer swallowed me whole the second I stepped inside. Marble floors gleamed under chandeliers that looked fit for palaces. Portraits lined the walls—men in suits, women in gowns, all bearing the same piercing Sinclair eyes. They seemed to watch me pass, silent judges in gilt frames. The butler's footsteps were soft, mine sharper, clicking like punctuation.

At the end of the hall, voices carried—low, polished, threaded with the kind of politeness that could cut sharper than raised tones.

The butler paused at the threshold, announcing me with crisp formality. "Ms. Noelle Collins."

CHAPTER 23

Pieces in Position

Ezra

It had been thirty-four days. I knew because I'd counted them—each one marked by the discipline of not reaching out, not circling back to her office like a man starved. Thirty-four days of Alexandra's name linked with mine until it felt less like news and more like branding. Thirty-four days of telling myself it didn't matter. She had made her choice. I had accepted it and moved accordingly.

Or I thought I had.

The estate buzzed with the sound of old money at ease. Laughter drifted from the great room where family friends mingled, glasses in hand, cold power wrapped in warm smiles. My mother's staff moved like clockwork—collecting empties, adjusting candles, keeping the evening on rails she'd laid out weeks ago.

It was all noise. Predictable. Until the butler's voice carried across the marble foyer.

"Ms. Noelle Collins."

The name cut through the room like a dropped glass.

Every head turned. Mine most of all.

And then she appeared.

She stepped in from the threshold, haloed by the chandelier's glow. Midnight silk moved like water against her frame, her hair catching the light in glossy spirals, her skin warm against marble and glass. She didn't rush, didn't shrink. She walked like she had every right to be here.

Conversation stumbled as she passed—men's eyes following too long, women measuring her with the kind of comparison they thought they hid well. She didn't flinch under it. Chin high, gaze steady, as if the scrutiny slid right off her.

But I saw the catch in my own chest, the one I'd spent thirty-four days trying to bury.

Noelle.

She wasn't supposed to be here. Which meant only one thing—my mother was involved. But none of that mattered in the moment. Because for the first time in weeks, the noise faded and I couldn't look away.

Every detail hit harder than it should have—the shine of her curls against the light, the slope of her collarbone above a thin line of jewelry, the steadiness in her eyes that once made me believe she saw through everything I pretended to be.

I hadn't realized how much I missed her until that second. Missed the sharp edges and the quiet truths. Missed the way she pulled me out of the façade I was living in and made the world feel real.

And I wasn't the only one who noticed. A man at my side muttered something under his breath before raising his glass. I gripped mine tighter, the cut of crystal biting into my palm.

She wasn't here for me. She was here because my mother had decided it. A pawn placed on the board.

Still—I wanted to close the space between us and say what I was too stubborn to say a month ago. My body leaned toward her before years of control dragged me back.

And then Mom's voice rose, clear and commanding above the chatter:

"Ladies and gentlemen, we are ready to move to the dining room for dinner—"

The spell snapped, but the ache didn't.

The dining room wasn't built for modest evenings. A table that stretched the length of the room, chandeliers blazing overhead, crystal and silver set like soldiers in formation. My father at the head, my mother beside him, the rest filled with partners, allies, and those who liked to pretend they were friends.

I took my seat and saw the card waiting: *Ezra Sinclair— Alexandra Martin.* Her name written neat as a contract. She slipped into the chair at my side.

Then my mother rose, her voice carrying just enough to reach our end of the table. "We're honored to have you tonight, Ms. Collins." She gestured to the empty chair across from me, as if it had been waiting all along.

Noelle sat with the same composure she carried into every room, silk sliding against the chair, perfume threading into the air. My siblings greeted her politely, my father gave a nod, my mother sat back satisfied.

No one else saw it, but I did. The fraction too long she smoothed her napkin. The small shift in her shoulders as she braced herself. My mother thought she was honoring her. What she'd really done was place her under fire.

Across the table, silver gleamed, wine glasses caught the glow, but all I felt was the pull of her presence.

At my side, Alexandra leaned in, her voice low. "We both know how this works. Our families approve. The press approves. We could make it official. Engagement, marriage. Clean. Simple."

Her tone wasn't harsh. Just matter-of-fact. Practicality dressed as inevitability.

But my eyes slid back to Noelle. The set of her jaw as she answered the man beside her. The smile that didn't quite reach. The way his interest lingered and eyes dragged across her face.

Something in me tightened, jealousy buried under a measured sip of wine. Alexandra was right—this should have been simple. But the second Noelle walked in, it wasn't.

My mother's voice carried again. "We may be witnessing the start of something promising tonight." Her gaze drifted toward Alexandra, then back to me. "Noelle has done remarkable work. An engagement may not be far off."

Glasses lifted. Polite applause circled the table. I raised mine because that was expected. But my eyes never left Noelle.

Malcolm leaned forward, smooth as ever. "Impressive, Ms. Collins. Matching Ezra couldn't have been easy."

Her reply was clipped. "It's what I do." Then she took a sip of her champagne.

He stared at her longer than he should have. My jaw locked.

And she still didn't look at me once. That was worse than if she had.

Julian, always ready to cut the tension, grinned. "Pickleball! That's where I know you from. Didn't think you had that kind of game."

Her lips curved faintly. "It was just a friendly match."

Before she could say more, my mother's voice slid in. "Oh? You've met before?"

"Yes," Noelle said evenly. "Briefly."

My mother's smile sharpened. "Well, however it happened, I'm grateful. Because what you've done is exceptional. Ezra and Alexandra—now that is a pairing. Legacy. Elegance. Everything aligned."

My father leaned back, satisfied. "Your mother's right. You've never looked this stable Ezra. Good to see."

Vivienne turned, smiling at Noelle. "And Alexandra's everywhere lately—the spreads, the galas. You must be happy it all worked out."

Alexandra smiled, her hand brushing mine lightly on the tablecloth before cutting back to Noelle. "I'm certainly grateful. Ms. Collins gave us the introduction. That kind of precision is rare."

To the others, it sounded gracious. To me, it was a claim. And Noelle felt it—her shoulders stiffened the slightest degree.

Malcolm smirked. "Rare's one word for it." His eyes cut across to her again, feeding on tension.

Julian, ever the jester, tipped his glass. "Come on, don't make it sound impossible. Though—" he grinned at Noelle— "if you got him to show up anywhere without protest, you deserve a medal."

Laughter broke around the table. Alexandra's included.

Not mine.

Because I couldn't stop watching her.

The table saw victory. The press calls it flawless. My mother saw control.

But I saw her—steady, elegant, and breaking in places only I would notice. The pause before she answered Alexandra. The way she clung to her water glass like it was safer than looking up. The flicker in her breath when my mother said *engagement*.

The table saw triumph.

But all I saw was her, holding herself together while the life I wish I hadn't chosen was paraded as her success.

And the longer she kept her eyes from mine, the more it felt like she'd chosen it too.

CHAPTER 24

The Study of Us

Noelle

The table hummed with conversation, rehearsed and effortless. It all blended into a single current, sound without substance, pulling me under even as I sat among them.

My smile stayed in place, smooth, unshaken, while inside I was fraying strand by strand. Evelyn's toast replayed like a broken record, each repetition pressing harder. A ring. Soon. My orchestration of the match paraded as a success story— while three feet away, Ezra sat beside Alexandra while trying to get my attention with a look he has always saved for me. I pretended I didn't see it.

I smoothed the napkin in my lap, already folded into faultless lines. My fingertips traced the fabric like I could anchor myself through texture, through repetition. But the more I held still, the closer I came to cracking.

I pushed my chair back, the legs gliding quiet over the floor. "Excuse me, where's your ladies' room?" My voice was steady, but my breath wasn't.

The butler appeared as if he'd been waitin, "Of course, Ms. Collins. This way."

I followed him through echoing halls, the din of the dining room dissolving with every step until marble silence swallowed it whole. The powder room was everything Sinclair money could buy—sprawling marble vanity, sconces casting warm light into gilded mirrors, fresh, vibrant orchids in crystal vases. Even the towels, monogrammed with the family crest, were folded with surgical precision. Luxury built to impress, even in solitude.

I stood at the mirror, fingertips grazing the cool edge, pretending to touch up lipstick that hadn't smeared. Anything to steady my hands. The chatter I'd left behind replayed in fragments—Evelyn's toast, Alexandra's laugh, her hand brushing Ezra's sleeve. My reflection stared back at me, flawless on the surface, but hollow-eyed. Like I'd stepped into someone else's body, wearing composure that didn't belong to me.

The door opened, hinges whispering against the hush. Footsteps followed—measured, unhurried.

"Noelle."

Her voice carried warmth stripped of audience polish. I turned slightly, catching her in the mirror before I faced her fully.

Vivienne.

Even away from the crowd, she carried that rare gracefulness—the kind you couldn't stage.

"I wanted to check on you," she said, plain and unadorned. "Dinner tables like that can feel like arenas."

I forced a smile that tasted more like survival than truth. "I'm fine."

Vivienne studied me in the mirror, head tilted, as if she could see through the veneer. "Maybe. But I've never seen my brother look at anyone the way he looked at you tonight."

The words hit harder than I wanted them to. My breath snagged, and I redirected my gaze to the orchids, the folded towels, anywhere but her reflection.

She stepped closer, voice gentling. "So tell me… are you really only the matchmaker here?"

Silence stretched, broken only by the muffled hum bleeding in from the hall. I opened my mouth, then shut it again, the professional answers I usually leaned on slipping out of reach.

Vivienne didn't press. She just rested a light hand on my arm, her bracelets brushing cool against my sleeve. "Whatever the truth is… I've never seen him like this before."

Before I could speak, the click of heels echoed toward us—sharp, decisive. The moment fractured.

Vivienne gave me one last look, steady and knowing, before sliding her socialite smile back into place. "We should go," she said gently.

But her words trailed me like a thread, winding tighter the closer we came to the door.

When I stepped back into the hall, the house pressed in with its own pulse. Laughter spilled from the great room, violins laced through the air, and crystal sang faintly as servers wove champagne trays through clusters of conversation. I caught one flute as a waiter passed. Then, without thinking, another. His brow arched, but he didn't break stride.

I slipped further from the crowd, letting the hush of a side corridor pull me in. The study opened like a reprieve—air thick with leather and wood polish, shelves stacked with gold-stamped spines. Lamplight flickered low and shadows collected in the corners. A room for confidences. Or for hiding.

I sank into a leather armchair, the glasses balanced against my knees. Evelyn's toast echoed in my mind. Alexandra's smile, radiant and merciless. Ezra's silence, the worst wound of all. It coiled inside me until I felt splintered from the inside out.

The first glass disappeared in three hard swallows, bubbles scraping down my throat. I set it aside on a desk and clutched the second like a security blanket, something to busy my hands when my thoughts threatened to spill through.

Leave, I told myself. Make an excuse—client call, early meeting, anything to protect the last shreds of composure and dignity. Better to escape before another toast, another round of applause, before I cracked wide open.

I shifted, bracing to stand—when movement snagged at the edge of my vision.

Ezra.

He stood framed in the doorway, searching the shadows like he'd been hunting me. His gaze drifted across the shelves, past the lamplight—until it found me.

The room shrank to silence. The chandeliers, the clinking glass, the orchestration of his mother's dinner—all of it fell away. Only the tick of a hidden clock remained, and the burn of his eyes on mine.

He stepped in, not close, but close enough that I could feel the his energy. Close enough that I caught the faint trace of his cologne, darker and sharper than memory had allowed. My pulse stuttered against the rim of my glass.

"You slipped away," he said, voice low, threaded with something rough.

"That's what exits are for." My tone cut sharper than I intended, a defense I didn't believe in.

His eyes flicked to the glass on the desk then to the one I still held. "Two drinks?"

"One's a primer." I lifted it slightly. "For… this."

His mouth curved—half-smile, half-surrender—but his eyes stayed locked on me, unguarded. "Effective?"

The laugh that escaped was thin, nervous. "Not even close."

He moved another step inside, careful but deliberate, until the lamplight touched the line of his jaw. He didn't cross the final distance, but it felt like he had. I could feel his presence vibrating through the quiet, tightening the air between us.

"I didn't expect to see you here," he said. No accusation— just raw truth.

"Neither did I." My voice was steady, but my grip whitened around the stem of my glass.

He watched me, every second stretching longer than it should. Then, softly, "Thirty-four days."

The words jolted through me. My eyes snapped to his.

"I kept count."

The admission hit like heat against my skin. My throat closed around the weight of it.

"You shouldn't say things like that."

"Why not?" His tone was even, but underneath was a fray I hadn't heard before—restraint stretched thin, ready to tear.

"Because…" I shook my head, quick, desperate. "Because it makes this harder than it already is."

His gaze searched mine, unrelenting, like he was trying to memorize me. My whole body felt alive under the scrutiny, every nerve sharpened by the fact that he hadn't touched me and yet I felt him everywhere.

"I don't regret a word from that office," he murmured. "Except maybe letting you end it."

The champagne trembled in my hand. I set it down too fast, glass clinking faintly against marble. My palms were bare now, useless, aching for something they couldn't reach.

"Ezra…" His name came out softer than I meant, cracked with something I didn't want him to hear. "Don't."

But he didn't move, and somehow that was worse. His eyes held mine, consuming me, like he was relearning me one detail at a time. I felt it in the heat of my chest, in the air that seemed too thin to draw into my lungs.

The silence stretched taut, a thread ready to snap. If he stepped closer, if I leaned even slightly forward, everything would unravel. And the truth was—I wanted him to.

Then footsteps rang down the corridor. Heels. A voice.

"There you are."

The spell shattered.

Vivienne stood in the doorway, composed smile, sharp eyes that caught everything in an instant. She looked between us once before turning to her brother.

"Ezra," she said lightly, though her gaze flicked back to me. "Alexandra's looking for you."

The blade was subtle, but it cut clean.

Ezra's jaw worked. He lingered one second longer than he should have, then nodded once, sharp, before retreating toward the noise of the great room.

Vivienne stayed. She stepped inside, studying me like a page she'd already read.

"It's good to see you again, Noelle," she said warmly, but there was weight under it. "You've left quite an impression."

"On who?" The question slipped out before I could stop it.

Her hand brushed my arm, her bracelets cool against my skin. "On him. On me. And impressions like that?" Her smile tilted, faint, knowing. "They don't fade."

She left me with that, the quiet click of the door sealing her words inside the study with me. I sank back into the chair, breath caught somewhere between dread and relief. Because Vivienne was right. Tonight hadn't just been a dinner. It had been a study—and I was no longer sure who was writing the notes.

CHAPTER 25

Salt and Fire on Water

Noelle

The office had been empty for hours, silence loud enough that every tick of the clock landed like a hammer. My lamp threw a pale circle across half-open folders, words I wasn't even seeing. I told myself I was working, but really, I was hiding—from the memory of Ezra Sinclair at that dinner, close enough to touch, untouchable all the same.

My phone buzzed against the desk, shattering the quiet. Unknown number. My thumb hovered, ready to ignore it.

"Ms. Collins."
The voice was low. Deep. Him.

I sat upright, pulse skittering. "Ezra?"

"Come downstairs."

Confusion consumed my face, "Excuse me?"

"You've been working all day. Let me thank you properly. The driver's waiting."

"Ezra, if this is about—"

Click. The line went dead.

Heat surged up my throat. The audacity. The nerve. And yet… I was already reaching for my bag.

The black car idled at the curb, headlights cutting through the night. The driver stepped out, my name spoken like a formality. The back door opened before I could think twice.

Inside, leather cool against my skin, I saw it: a short glass of scotch in the holder, a folded card propped beside it. His handwriting—spare, deliberate, stripped of flourish.

Indulge me.

I should've said no. Should've sent the driver away. Instead, I let the city blur by, streetlights flickering across my reflection, and said nothing.

The marina was hushed when we pulled in, water shifting against the docks in low rhythm. His yacht waited—lit soft along its edges. Not ostentatious. Commanding.

He stood at the rail, jacket gone, sleeves rolled, the night wind tugging at his shirt. No cameras. No audience. Just Ezra Sinclair, stripped of armor, framed by the dark water.

"You came." Not smug. Not surprised. Relieved.

I climbed the gangway, heels careful against the boards. "I assumed this was business."
"Not tonight." He poured two glasses, handed one to me, fingers brushing mine. "This is thanks."
"For what?"
"For putting up with me. For being right."

I laughed under my breath, sharp, disbelieving. "About Alexandra?"
His gaze held mine. "That's what I should say."

The bourbon burned smooth, but it was nothing compared to the silence between us. The kind that thickened until it filled every space.

"Ezra, this isn't a good idea."
"That depends," he said, leaning against the rail, eyes fixed on me. "On what you want it to be."

***

For a while, we stayed light. His brother's antics. My client who only dated between baseball seasons. Things that made him laugh—the kind of laugh you couldn't fake. And for a few minutes, it was too easy.

Which is why I ruined it.

"Congratulations," I said, tighter than I meant. "You and Alexandra seem… well-suited."

His glass stilled halfway to his lips. Then he looked at me, really looked, and the temperature between us changed. "That's what you think?"

"It's what everyone thinks. She's graceful. Polished. The kind of woman who doesn't flinch in a ballroom."
His mouth curved faintly. "That sounded rehearsed."

"It's not." My grip tightened on the rail. "It's—"

"Safe," he cut in, voice low, sharp. "Safe is just another word for alone."

I turned to the water slipping black under the hull. "You're imagining things."

"I see the way you look at me, Noelle." He'd moved closer without me noticing, heat brushing against my skin. "Even across the dinner table. Don't tell me it was nothing."

The words caught in my throat. Evelyn's voice intruded anyway: *This is the kind of woman my son needs.*

"Some things don't survive daylight," I whispered. "Not in your world. Not in mine. Even your mother made that clear."

His head tilted. "My mom? About Alexandra?"

"About the kind of woman you're supposed to marry."

His jaw worked. His eyes darkened. "So it wasn't just in my head."

I tried to step past him, but his fingers brushed mine— light, careful, stopping me cold.

You hide behind jokes and your rules," he murmured. His eyes caught mine, steady but raw. "But all I see is the way you hold yourself too tight, like letting go for even a second would cost you everything."

The truth sliced too close. If anyone ever pulled at those threads, traced me back to where I came from, everything I'd built *could* unravel.

"I can't afford to take certain kinds of risks." My voice shook.

"And yet you're here."

I made the mistake of looking up. His eyes locked on mine, and everything fractured.

The first brush of his mouth undid me. The second was fire. I kissed him back with everything I'd buried, fists clutching at his shirt like I needed proof he was real.

His hand slid to my waist, pulling me closer, reckless and inevitable. My body screamed yes while my mind whispered run.

The kiss should've been enough. But it wasn't.

"Ezra…" My lips trembled against his. "This isn't—"
He froze, muscles taut, breath harsh. But he didn't let go.

"Say it," he whispered. "If you want me to stop, I stop. But if you don't—" his thumb brushed the edge of my ribs, light enough to burn "—then I need to hear it."

The waves lapped constantly, my pulse matching them. I opened my mouth, truth spilling out. "I want this."

His forehead pressed to mine, eyes searching. "Tell me what you want."

My body answered before my mouth did, arching toward him, fingers digging into his shirt. When the words came, they were clear.

"You. I want you."

Something in him broke. The restraint snapped. His mouth crashed back onto mine, hotter, hungrier, and I met him with everything I'd buried.

The night blurred into heat and confession, the sea rocking beneath us. And when his voice rasped against my ear—"Stay with me tonight"—I didn't answer with words. My body said it all.

Later, curled against him on the deck, whispers slipped out we'd never intended to share.

He told me about his family—the distance, the way every conversation circled money and business. How only Julian still saw *him* instead of head of Sinclair Holdings.

And I told him about my mother's illness, about my brother, Cal, across the map, about how absence sometimes felt like betrayal no matter how much love existed underneath.

He didn't try to fix it. He just listened, intently. The kind of silence that let me breathe deeper than I had in months.

When my head tipped onto his shoulder, I started to pull back. But his arm curved around me, sure and protective, as though it belonged there. And the sea rocked me into sleep.

***

The yacht glided toward the dock, sunlight spilling gold across the water. I blinked awake to find his arm still draped over me, his gaze fixed on the horizon.

"Morning," he said, voice rough.

"Morning."

For a while, neither of us moved. Then his voice broke the quiet.

"I haven't felt this right in a long time…"

The words hit sharp. My throat tightened. "Ezra…"

He turned to me, eyes unflinching. "Say you don't feel the same. If you can, I'll let you walk off this boat and we'll never speak of it again."

I opened my mouth, but the protest stuck. The truth burned. Instead, I laid my head on his shoulder.

His mouth curved and he put his arm around me, "That's what I thought."

He dipped his chin, voice low at my temple. "For the record, I'm officially ending our contract with you as my matchmaker. I'll email Sadie tonight and settle it."

"What about the deadline? And your parents?"

"I am Sinclair Holdings. I've carried this company farther than any deadline ever could. Let me handle them. You handle deciding if you want this—with me."

The hush after was worse than any argument.

"We'll dock in a few minutes," he said finally, tone clipped back into formality. "The driver's waiting." A pause. "Thank you for coming and staying."

I nodded once, unable to trust my voice. Each step toward the pier felt like walking against the pull of a tide. The salt air clung sharp in my lungs, whispering the truth I didn't want to name:

Whatever line we thought we hadn't crossed, we already had.

And there was no undoing it.

CHAPTER 26

Over-Exposed

Ezra

The office was quiet, but for once it didn't feel suffocating. The skyline stretched past the glass, towers burning like a constellation, and for the first time in longer than I could remember, I let myself breathe in it.

I should've been buried in numbers, but my mind had already betrayed me—wandering back to her.

Noelle.

The way her voice softened when she finally spoke truths I knew she rarely shared. The way her shoulders eased, as though she'd shrugged off a weight only she could feel. And then—her against me. Head on my shoulder. Breath steadying as she drifted to sleep with my arm still holding her.

It wasn't just closeness. It was trust. The kind she didn't hand out carelessly. Her warmth pressed into me, the faint thread of her perfume lingering in the salt air, the brush of her hair against my jaw every time the boat rocked. Hours later, my body still remembered it—the shape of her, the pull of tilting my head just enough to kiss the curve where her neck met her shoulder.

She didn't open up easily. But that night, she had. Not only her smile. Not only her guard. She gave me a nearness that couldn't be mistaken for anything but real feelings, even if neither of us dared name it.

And now the memory clung like fire. The silk of her skin beneath my hand. The heat of her lips when she finally kissed me back. How quickly desire had rooted once it was given air.

I'd lived surrounded by abundance. But I'd never known hunger or warmth like this.

The buzz of my phone cut through, sharp as glass against the desk.

I reached for it absently, still half lost in her. Expecting Vivienne. A report. Something routine.

Instead, words flashed across the screen:

You might want to be more careful.

And beneath it, a photo.

My chest locked tight. Noelle asleep against me, my arm curved around her. Real. Intimate. Never meant for anyone's eyes but ours. Now stripped bare, weaponized.

I snapped the screen dark, but the image seared hotter behind my lids. From a high angle. Not a phone from the deck. Drone? How many more angles?

My thumb hovered over my security chief's number, but a knock broke the moment. My assistant leaned in, composed as ever.

"Mr. Sinclair, the board is waiting."

I slid the phone into my pocket. Tie straightened. Mask back on. But inside, the storm was already rising.

***

The boardroom hummed with its usual rhythm—charts, dry voices, papers smoothed by old money hands.

Which is why I didn't see it coming.

Malcolm cleared his throat mid-update, voice silked with calculation. "Before we move forward," he said, sliding a folder onto the table, "there's a matter of public optics."

I barely looked up, expecting another shallow market report. But then he fanned the folder open, spreading photographs like a dealer laying down a winning hand.

The air shifted. Chairs creaked. A low murmur rolled the length of the table.

And there it was.

Noelle. Her head resting on my shoulder, my arm claiming her as though it belonged there. Another frame—sunset across the yacht, champagne flutes, her laughter caught like light itself.

My breath caught, a second too slow.

Of course it was Malcolm. The opportunist. He's always circling, waiting to claim what was never his. And now he'd chosen to strike.

Dad's pen stilled. His eyes lifted—cool, surgical. "Ezra," he said, each syllable a scalpel, "would you care to explain?"

I kept my expression even while my pulse hammered. "Where did you get these?" My voice was low, edged.

Malcolm smiled, smug as a cat with cream. "Where isn't the point. What matters is the impression. Our CEO flaunting—" his hand flicked toward Noelle's face, dismissive, obscene "—companions outside the bounds of discretion. Reckless. Destabilizing."

The word companions cut deep. She wasn't some nameless diversion. And she sure as hell wasn't his to belittle.

"She's not the subject here," I said, voice flat but laced with steel. "Dragging her name into this room to score points says more about you than it does about me."

A few directors shifted uneasily. My father didn't blink.

Malcolm leaned back, smile widening. "It says I care about the company's future. Image matters, Ezra. If you can't keep your private life contained, how can we trust you with Sinclair's?"

We? He's not even a Sinclair. The audacity. Twisting intimacy into liability. Love into leverage. Wait…love?

I gathered my notes. No crack for him to savor. "If this is the best use of our time," I said, voice blade-thin, "then the meeting is over."

Gasps. A chair scraped. I didn't look back.

My phone buzzed again in my pocket as I walked out. More photos. More poison.

And beneath the fury, one truth blazed:

He wasn't just coming for me.

He was coming for her.

***

The door shut behind me with a thud that rattled bone.

I didn't head for my office—too many eyes, too many whispers. Instead, I cut down the private hall, into the corner conference room, empty but for its wide window over the city.

The skyline glittered, glass and steel pretending it had answers. My reflection didn't. It looked like a man split in two.

The phone lit with fresh pings. More photos. Different angles. Noelle laughing, hair loose, champagne in her hand. My arm at her back. A tenderness I hadn't realized the world could see.

My stomach hollowed.

I could weather this storm. I'd been bred in storms. Let them question my judgment, my leadership, my name. I'd faced worse.

But Noelle?

Her name dragged through their mouths, her image reduced to liability? Malcolm twisting her into something cheap? I'd burn the company down before I let that happen.

I pressed the phone to my forehead, forcing breath past the knot in my chest.

She had trusted me. Trusted me enough to fall asleep against me, to lay down her armor. And I hadn't protected her.

My jaw tightened. That would be the last time.

I slid the phone into my pocket, squared my shoulders, and stared out at the city until the reflection staring back wasn't shaken anymore.

They wanted her?

They'd have to deal with me first.

CHAPTER 27

Double-Edged

Noelle

The first call came just after ten.

"Ms. Collins?" The man's voice was flat, formal. "We've decided to terminate our contract, effective immediately."

My pen stilled over the page. "Terminate?"

"It isn't personal. Strictly… appearances." His words snapped off like lines he'd been handed and told to read.

The line clicked dead.

One client. Manageable, I told myself. I set the receiver down slowly, as if careful motion could calm the thud in my chest.

The second call arrived before I could lift the pen.

"Ms. Collins, I'm sorry to inform you—"

I didn't need the rest. Another polite goodbye. My throat tightened; my reply came out smooth, automatic, the voice I'd practiced for years. "Thank you for letting me know."

By the third call, the coffee at my elbow had gone cold. Three clients. Three of my biggest. Gone before noon.

Outside my glass walls, the office hummed—keyboards, low conference voices, the ordinary churn of business-as-usual. Inside my office the silence pressed in, thick and hard.

I walked to the window. Houston spread out below, towers glittering. For years I read those buildings as proof that grit could build an empire. Today they felt like sentries— indifferent, immovable.

My palm flattened against the glass. Every late night, every compromise, every careful choice—undone in a single morning. This wasn't coincidence.

It was a message. And I didn't yet know who'd sent it.

Raised voices filtered through my door. Sadie's tone, clipped: "Ms. Martin, I'm sorry, but Ms. Collins is in the middle of work. If you'll schedule an appointment—"

"Work can wait," Alexandra's voice replied—demanding, dismissive. "This is urgent."

The door nudged. Sadie planted herself in the frame like a human barricade. Behind her, Alexandra stood perfectly composed: black sheath, immaculate hair, a smile sharpened into a weapon.

Sadie shot me a look. "Do you want me to call security or—"

"It's fine," I said, though my stomach dropped. "Let her in."

Reluctantly, Sadie stepped aside. Alexandra's heels clicked across the floor like punctuation.

"You always were gracious," she murmured, dropping her clutch onto my desk with a loud snap. She pushed a cream envelope forward with a manicured finger. "Go on. See what happens when private indulgences become public evidence. I received these anonymously this morning."

A chill crawled up my spine before I even opened it. My hands moved anyway.

The photos spilled out like accusations. Ezra's arm around me on the yacht. My head on his shoulder. Laughter, sunset, champagne—moments that had been ours, now frozen for strangers to judge.

My breath hitched. The morning's phone calls aligned themselves in my head. Not accident. Not guiltless coincidence. Her.

"That isn't what it looks like," I whispered, weak and useless.

Alexandra's smile widened, perfumed and practiced. "Of course it isn't. It never is. But perception doesn't care, darling." She tapped a photo with a nail. "How long do you think your business lasts when clients believe the matchmaker wanted the prize for herself? Taking advantage of your clients. What kind of businesswoman are you?"

My chest tightened. I could already hear the gossip, the way Houston legends morph a moment into a narrative. Noelle Collins—professional, discreet—reframed as the woman who'd blurred the rules.

"You think mothers will keep trusting you with their sons after this?" Alexandra asked, leaning in. Her voice was soft but sharp. "That women who hire you for discretion won't run at the first whiff of scandal? All it takes is one whisper."

I braced my hands on the desk. "Why are you here?" I asked.

"Because I'm giving you the courtesy of a choice." Her tone mellowed, rendering the cruelty polite. "Back away from Ezra. Quietly. Or I dismantle you loudly."

Her words lodged like glass.

The door opened then.

Ezra stepped in. His eyes scanned the room—first Alexandra, then the photos on my desk, then me. Shock flared, shifted to controlled fury.

"Alexandra, where did you get this from and why are you here," he said, clipped.

She turned with the same seamless composure. "Ezra. Perfect timing. I was just discussing brand risk with Ms. Collins. Someone has to think about your future. Ms. Collins here is learning her lesson with cancellations."

He closed the distance between us, the air tightening. "So your reaction is threatening her business? Dragging her reputation through the dirt?"

Alexandra arched a brow. "Reputation is everything. You should understand that."

Something in him snapped. He didn't shout; he didn't need to. His voice dropped low, every word a blade. "Don't you ever speak about her like that again."

The room went electric. For the first time, Alexandra's smile faltered.

Ezra reached across my desk, gathered the photographs into a neat stack, and pushed them back toward her. "You want to come for me—fine. But if you come for her," his eyes bore into Alexandra's, steel-hard, "you'll regret it."

It wasn't a loud threat. It didn't have to be. It pulsed in the air and settled there.

Alexandra's composure thinned. She slipped the photos into her clutch with a forced smile. "This isn't over," she said, voice thin as she turned to leave.

The door closed behind her. Her perfume hovered—a sweet, poisonous film.

My hands trembled. I dug my nails into my palms until half-moons bloomed. Pain was a welcome, reassuring proof of being alive.

Everything I'd built—late nights, cold calls, negotiations—was suddenly fragile because a few photos had been thrown like grenades across my desk. Alexandra was right: perception leaps before facts.

And the truth about my foundation wasn't flawless. It never had been.

Outside the tidy origin story people liked to tell—little-girl-with-a-plan, self-made, relentless—was a buried fact I'd kept hidden: my brother. He'd helped me get started. The routes he used, the clients he'd introduced—some of it had come from corners that didn't advertise. He trafficked in art that didn't always have provenance; his world was velvet-lined backrooms and unmarked vaults.

If anyone pulled that thread, the narrative would rip. Self-made would become suspect. Visionary would become compromise. They'd find the messy parts of my past and brand me something else entirely.

Panic hit bright and hot. I pressed my palm to my forehead, trying to stop the world tilting.

"You should go," I said, voice gone raw.

Ezra didn't move.

"I mean it," I said, more brittle. "This is already bad enough without you standing here, reminding me how I let it happen. Just—leave."

He stepped closer instead.

"Noelle." His voice was soft but sure, like an anchor in sound. "I'm not going anywhere."

A jagged laugh burst from me. "You don't understand. She doesn't have to do much. All she has to do is point. And if someone starts looking—" I couldn't finish. The shame tasted acid in my mouth.

He didn't blink. "Then let them dig," he said, blunt and cold. "Whatever they find doesn't erase who you are or what you've built."

But he didn't know. He couldn't know the specifics, the places the dirt had been covered with quick hands and promises. I shook my head; a sob tore loose.

"You can't protect me from this. Not from them. Not from what I've done." My confession fell on the carpet between us.

Ezra's jaw tightened. The shadow in his eyes set like iron. "Watch me," he said.

It wasn't defiance. It was resolve—heavy and certain.

And the worst part was how much I wanted to believe him. The want it stirred felt like betrayal to my fear.

I turned away and wiped my face hard.

"Ezra, please—" I started.

His hand hovered near mine, a solid presence rather than pressure. "Look at me."

I did.

What I found wasn't pity or performance. It was hard, clear certainty and protection—fierce, plain.

"You're not going to face this alone," he said, quieter but absolute. "Not ever."

The panic didn't vanish. It slowed. It became something tethered to one stubborn, impossible truth:

If the walls fell, he was choosing to stand inside them with me.

Crystal Clear

Ezra

The truth crystallized the moment I stepped into Noelle Collins's office and saw Alexandra scattering photographs like evidence, slicing at Noelle's reputation with the same cool precision Evelyn would have used. Alexandra Martin hadn't just played her part; she'd drawn blood.

Watching Noelle hold her ground while Alexandra picked her apart, I felt it—the break, the clarity.

This wasn't a match. It was a transaction.

The Martins and Sinclairs have orbited each other for decades—contracts signed, hands shaken at galas. On paper, Alexandra and I made sense. Palatable. Practical. A merger in couture. But what I saw today stripped the gloss away.

I'd known of her, of course. Everyone in Houston did. Alexandra Martin: luminous, camera-ready, a family name etched into the city's architecture. Since the match, though, the seams were showing—the calculation behind every smile, the strategy in every casual touch, the way she echoed my mother. Polished. Tactical. Ruthless.

I don't need another woman like my mother steering my life.

I found Alexandra where I knew she'd be—St. Regis bar, the Martins' corner table, a crystal glass sweating in her hand. Black dress, hair in a chignon sharp enough to cut, her reflection multiplied in the mirror behind her.

She didn't flinch when I sat. If anything, her mouth curved the way it does for photographs. "I wondered how long it would take you."

"I'm not here to wonder."

She tipped her glass, the ice catching light. "Then you're here to scold me again. You were very clear in Ms. Collins's office."

The name hit harder than she meant it to. My jaw tightened. "Look, I came here to have a conversation."

Her brows lifted, but she let it go. "You think I enjoyed it? Marching in there, playing the villain? Don't insult me, Ezra. I was hurt. I was matched with you, paraded with you, written into your family's narrative like a sure thing. And all the while—" her voice sharpened "—you wanted her."

I didn't deny it. Lying would've been cruelty layered over insult.

"I never promised you love," I said, leaning in, even. "We both knew what this was: two families tying a tighter knot. We agreed to the image."

Her fingers tightened on the glass; a crack of heat slipped through the polish. "Maybe. But I started to think it could be more. You were… not what I expected. Not soft. Not cold." A brittle laugh. "It doesn't matter."

For a beat, I almost saw her—not the heir, not my mother's mirror, but a woman weighing what vulnerability would cost.

I didn't soften. "It mattered enough for you to walk into her office and cut her down."

She bristled. I kept going.

"I've seen that brand of precision before. The smile that opens a vein. It's my mother's best trick. And Alexandra"—my voice held—"I'm not marrying my mother."

It landed. She masked it, but not fast enough.

"Technically," I said after a beat, "we never confirmed anything. It was speculation—dinners, appearances." I let it sit. "Which means this can still be clean."

Suspicion flickered. I laid it out.

"You say we were discussing a joint venture. That's all. If you want it to stick, I'll sit with your father and put something on paper—numbers, contracts, something real. When the questions come—and they will—you save face. You weren't left. You were in control."

Her mouth curved—not a smile. "You make it sound neat."

"It is, if you take it. Quietly."

"And if I don't?"

"Then I let the story spin as is—that you chased a man who was never yours, that the Martins pressed for a union I never agreed to, that you tried to destroy the reputation of a woman who's done you no harm." I leaned in, calm steel. "And I make sure every boardroom and country club in this city hears it."

Her breath caught; fury flashed and vanished. She's not reckless. She's trained to survive.

"You think you've boxed me in."

"No," I said. "I'm giving you an exit."

We held the stare. She weighed pride against cost, then knocked back her drink, set the glass down with a clean clink, and smoothed her dress.

"I'll handle it," she said at last. Clipped. Pride bruised. Calculations turning behind her eyes. She knew it was the smart move.

I learned the difference between standing next to a man and being with him," she said, rotating the glass. "Thank you for the lesson."

She rose, gathering her clutch, chin high. "Don't mistake this for mercy, Ezra. The Martins don't forget."

"Neither do I."

Her heels clicked across marble; her perfume lingered like smoke. I let out one slow breath. Not victory. Not relief. Clarity.

And clarity said this: Alexandra Martin wasn't the kind of danger that could undo me. But Evelyn was right about one thing—optics matter. From now on, every move with Noelle would carry the weight of a war.

***

The news hit before I was out of bed.

Her post was surgical—succinct, measured, unassailable:

"After thoughtful discussion, Ezra and I have decided not to move forward with the joint venture we'd been exploring. Our recent meetings were about business, not romance. Ezra has always been a trusted friend, and that's all we've ever been. I encourage everyone not to give weight to unfounded rumors in blogs or tabloids. I wish him continued success and am excited for what's ahead."

No photographs. No Noelle. A clean incision. Exactly what I asked for.

The comments were predictable: See? You can't trust blogs. Not every man and woman photographed together are a couple. Business ≠ romance.

Relief didn't come. Stones in my chest did. I hadn't won anything. I'd bought time.

By noon, my phone buzzed again—my mother's voice, clipped: "Come now."

The house smelled like roses—fresh arrangements in every room. The air was too still, as if the walls were bracing. I found her in the sunroom, posture immaculate, blinds tilted to ration the light.

She didn't stand. She didn't have to. Her gaze pinned me where I was.

"I thought we agreed on this plan," she said, soft but edged. "And now you've backed out. What do we do with the timeline? The deadline is only a few months away."

I closed the door; the click sounded loud. "I told you. I'm handling my life on my own."

"It is not yours alone to handle." Her voice wavered—barely. Then the slip, unguarded: "I don't have the time to watch you squander everything. I'm sick, Ezra."

Air left my lungs. The room widened and narrowed at once. My mother—unyielding, unflinching—was sick.

I moved closer, throat tight. "What do you mean?"

She lifted her chin, as if posture could hold back the truth. "I don't want people to take from you what we've worked so hard for. I wanted you on solid ground—if it was the last thing I did."

I crouched in front of her. "How long?"

Her eyes—usually glass—softened for a heartbeat. "A few years, if I'm lucky."

I broke. I took her hand. "Mom…" The word cracked; I hadn't used it in years.

For a second she was rigid. Then her hand slid to the back of my neck and she let me hold her. For the first time since I was a boy, she let me.

"I'll do whatever it takes," I said into her hair. "I'll protect what we built. I'll keep my seat. But I'll do it my way—not theirs. Not with sacrifices I can't live with. Trust me."

Her breath hitched. When she pulled back, there was the faintest sheen in her eyes, blinked away. She nodded once—small, careful. Not surrender. Something closer to trust.

I kissed her temple. "We'll face this together. But let me lead this time."

The quiet that followed felt fragile, almost tender. Roses perfumed the air. For once there were no commands, no verdicts—just a tremor in my mother's armor and my vow to carry it with her.

***

Evelyn

The echo of his footsteps lingered long after the door shut. Each one rang through the marble like punctuation I hadn't approved. For years, Ezra's steps had been mine to direct. I set the rhythm, and he kept it. Tonight, he chose his own.

And I let him.

I sat very still, my hand smoothing the silk of my dress where it had bunched under my grip. Discipline had always been my armor—if I held myself together, then everything else would follow. That had been my lesson to him since boyhood: control the image, control the outcome. Ezra absorbed it like scripture. Even when he bristled, he obeyed. Even when he doubted, he delivered. Our contract had been unspoken but absolute: I prepared the path, he walked it.

Until tonight.

His words still burned in the air: *I'll figure out how to do it my way.*

I should have felt rage. But beneath the sting, there was something unexpected. Pride. My son had stood in front of me, no longer a boy maneuvered by my hand, but a man making his own declarations. There was power in that, even if he didn't yet know how to wield it.

I rose from my chair and crossed to the window. Outside, the roses bloomed in disciplined rows, cut and trained to grow as they should. I touched the glass, watching the precise symmetry I demanded from the gardeners season after season. Perfection came from pruning. From shaping. Ezra was my strongest bloom—but even the strongest needed guidance. He thought he had shaken free, but roots don't detach so easily. He was still mine, still Sinclair, whether he liked it or not.

And yet… I saw it. The spark in his eyes, the steadiness in his voice. He was finally becoming his own man. Perhaps this was the moment I had been preparing him for all along.

But I knew better than to confuse manhood with mastery. He thought clarity was courage. He thought choosing for himself was enough. It wasn't. The world is crueler than that. It will slice at his weaknesses, and love—the kind that makes men reckless—is the sharpest knife of all.

I pressed harder against the glass, smudging my own reflection. *Noelle Collins.* I'd seen it in the way he looked at her, the flicker of something I couldn't train out of him. That girl had been allowed too close. Ezra believed it was love. I knew it was distraction. Love blurred judgment, weakened legacy, made men believe they were invincible until the fall came.

Still, I will not strike first. That has never been my way. Mistakes always reveal themselves, and when hers comes, I'll be waiting. Watching. Ready to pull Ezra back into place before he loses what we've built.

I breathed deep, the perfume of roses sharp in the air. "Go on, Ezra," I whispered. "Be your own man. But don't think for a moment I've stepped aside. I'll be here, ensuring it all still runs as it should."

The city lights blinked beneath me, bowing as they always had. Ezra thought he had claimed freedom tonight. What he didn't yet understand was that freedom has limits. And I have spent a lifetime defining them.

CHAPTER 29

Match of a Lifetime

Noelle

For weeks, I threw myself into work, into silence, into anything that wasn't Ezra Sinclair. I dodged his calls. Deleted his texts before I could reread them into meaning. Told myself if I stayed busy enough, if I stayed invisible enough, maybe the storm would pass.

But the tension wound tighter anyway — a coil in my chest that wouldn't ease.

So when the charity pickleball tournament rolled around, I signed up. Not because I cared about winning, but because I needed to move. To sweat. To hit something that would bounce back instead of break.

The courts were alive with color and chatter — sneakers squeaking, paddles cracking against plastic balls, laughter ringing from the bleachers. I tied my hair up, tightened my grip on the paddle, and told myself this was normal. Safe. A world where no one cared who I matched or who I might have kissed under the weight of a thousand stars.

I was halfway through warmups when I heard it — a voice I knew too well. Low. Commanding. Smooth as bourbon.

"Need a partner?"

My body stilled before my mind caught up. Slowly, I turned.

Ezra stood at the edge of the court, paddle in hand, dressed down in a simple tee and shorts. The image was almost disarming — no boardroom armor, no polished façade. Just a man who looked like he'd been waiting for me.

My chest tightened. "What are you doing here?"

His mouth curved, not quite a smile. "Same as you. Blowing off steam." He twirled the paddle easily in his hand. "And if I'm lucky, finding someone worth playing with."

I gripped my paddle harder, fighting the heat rising in my skin. "You shouldn't be here."

"Neither should you," he said, stepping onto the court like it was his natural place. His gaze locked on mine, unflinching. "But here we are."

The ref called for doubles partners. Without waiting for my consent, Ezra held out his hand — patient, daring me to refuse.

Around us, the chatter swelled, players swapping sides, the match about to begin.

I should have walked away. Should have let him stand there with his paddle and his persistence.

But instead, my hand found his.

And just like that, the game began — not just pickleball, but whatever this was between us, sharp and electric and impossible to keep contained.

Every serve, every return, every quick step across the painted lines synced like we'd practiced for years. He anticipated me, moved with me, covered where I left gaps. And when our arms brushed, when his hand steadied me at the small of my back after a close volley, it felt like more than a game.

"Nice save," he murmured once, low enough that only I could hear.

My chest tightened. "Don't read into it."

But the smirk tugging at his mouth said he already had.

By the final point, sweat slicked my skin, my laughter rang out unbidden, and his grin — real, unguarded — nearly undid me. We won, of course. The crowd clapped, players congratulated, and yet all I felt was the weight of his eyes on me, heavy and unrelenting.

The match was over. The applause faded. But my pulse still raced like the game hadn't stopped.

Ezra followed me to the sideline, his presence as close as my shadow.

"You've been avoiding me," he said.

I uncapped my water bottle, forcing the tremor from my hands. "I've been busy."

His gaze cut through the lie. "Noelle."

My throat tightened. "I can't do this."

His jaw flexed. He stepped closer, voice low and rough. "Then hear this. I ended it with Alexandra, and she's backing off your business."

The bottle slipped in my grip, water spilling across the concrete. I stared at him, breath snagging. "You… what?"

"She already made a statement saying it was all business, no romance." His eyes held mine, fierce and unrelenting. "Because I tried to let you go. I tried to bury it, to play the man everyone expected me to be, but every time I close my eyes,

it's you. Every room I walk into, I look for you. And I can't—"
He looked deep into my eyes. "I love you, Noelle."

The world narrowed. The laughter, the games, the players
— gone. Just his voice and the thundering in my chest.

I shook my head, tears burning hot. "You don't
understand. This could destroy me. My reputation. My work.
Everything I've spent years building."

He leaned in, close enough that the heat of him wrapped
around me. "I am not asking you to give up your business. If
anything I want to do whatever I can to protect everything and
everyone you care about. Because I love you."

The words lodged in my throat, jagged and unbearable. I
wanted to run. To hide. But his eyes wouldn't let me.

"I can't…deny it anymore," I whispered.

His breath caught. "Say it, Noelle."

Somewhere a phone lifted. A hush rippled along the
sideline

My heart thundered, every wall I'd built crumbling. "I love
you too," I said, voice raw, breaking. "I've tried to fight it. I've
tried to make it make sense. But I am in love with you, Ezra."

For a moment, the air between us was electric, suspended. Then his hand cupped the back of my neck, not pulling me in, not yet — just holding me.

"I want to be with you," he said, his voice rough with truth. "And I don't care what it costs me."

The words tore through me, terrifying and undeniable.

We stood there, two people who'd finally stopped lying to themselves — and with no idea what the world would do to us next.

PART IV

THE LIGHT

CHAPTER 30

Blood and Reputation

Ezra

The Sinclair boardroom wasn't built for mercy. The walnut table ran like a runway to my father's chair; the crest on the wall did the talking. Twelve directors sat around it, signatures sharp enough to move markets. At the head sat my father, the Sinclair crest carved into the wall above him like judgment itself.

I had delivered results here for years. Closed deals. Carried the name without complaint. But I had never asked for anything. Not once.

Until now.

"I'm requesting an extension." My voice was even, but it carried. "Two additional months on the deadline."

The silence that followed was sharp, the kind that prickles the skin. Harrington, the eldest director, scoffed. "You have three months left. Asking for more looks like doubt."

A stir rippled through the room — pens tapping, papers shifting, eyes turning my way with the same hunger they'd turned on weaker men.

Malcolm leaned in, cufflinks catching the light, his smile honed like a blade. "This isn't about scheduling. It's about reputation. Right now, Ezra looks distracted. Indecisive. And when a Sinclair heir wavers in public, the family image fractures. That kind of weakness bleeds into every deal we touch."

The photographs. The rumors. He didn't have to say them — the poison was already in the air.

My father's gaze cut through the noise, sharp enough to flay. "Why the delay?"

"Because I won't be cornered," I said, my tone neutral. "I want to do this right. This is a serious matter. Two more months gives me the stability and room I need to do that — for the family, and for the company."

Malcolm chuckled low, venom dripping. "Stability? Or stalling?"

The word sliced deeper than his smirk. Stalling. My father's disappointment wrapped in another man's voice.

Heat burned under my ribs. "Stalling is standing still. This is foresight. Two months isn't indulgence. It's discipline."

The directors murmured louder now, the tide pulling against me. For the first time, I felt it — the chair slipping beneath me.

And then—

"Enough."

The word cracked across the room.

Julian.

He leaned forward, elbows braced, eyes locked on Malcolm. No grin. No charm. Just unflinching fire.

"Malcolm, don't dress this up. This isn't about a timeline. It's about Ezra. And while you circle his reputation, let's not forget he's the one who's kept this company above water the last five years."

The silence that followed was instant. Heavy.

Julian had always spoken up for me — in boardrooms, at dinners, even in hushed hallways where no one dared challenge my father. It shouldn't have surprised me. And yet, in this room, surrounded by men who would rather see me bleed than bend, his voice was the only one that didn't feel like a knife.

He went on. "Weakness isn't asking for time. Weakness is chasing appearances while execution slips. Ezra isn't weak.

He's the one who holds the line. If he says he needs two more months, I think it's the least we can do."

My chest tightened with the weight of knowing he was, as always, the only sibling who stood beside me.

My father's gaze swung back to me, weighing heir against liability, son against standard. The pause stretched long enough that my breath hitched, long enough for every director at the table to measure the silence against me.

Finally, he exhaled, slow and sharp.
"Two more months. No more. You want the extension? Deliver Meridian. Fail, and you don't just lose the engagement. You lose this table and it goes to Vivienne."

The verdict struck like a gavel.

Across the table, Vivienne's nail clicked once against crystal, then went still.

The directors rose, chairs scraping. Some nodded, others looked away. My freedom was not granted. It was collateral.

Malcolm's smirk lingered, venomous, a promise of war.

Julian stayed seated, meeting my gaze with the same nod he'd given me a hundred times before.

Not victory. But not a loss either.

Just a countdown and brother-in-law counting on me to fail.

CHAPTER 31
The Art of Ruin

Malcolm

The door slammed behind me, the sound rattling through the glass walls of my office. The fury I'd kept leashed in the boardroom finally broke free. My hand closed around the crystal paperweight on my desk — a commemorative piece etched with the Sinclair crest — and I hurled it hard against the wall. It shattered in a spray of glass, a thousand fragments glittering on the floor like the company's fractured priorities.

Ezra. Always Ezra.

He'd sat there, calm as ever, asking for indulgences like a king handing out decrees. And they'd given it to him. Two months. Because Julian — the little brother who'd never carried a day's weight in his life — had decided to play savior.

"Pathetic," I muttered, my chest heaving.

Two of my staff stood frozen by the door, their eyes wide but mouths shut. The third, a wiry man in an ill-fitted suit, flinched when I turned on him.

"You," I snapped, pointing at him. "You thought a few yacht photos would be enough? That grainy shots of Sinclair holding some woman would topple him?"

He stammered. "W-we thought it would call his judgment into question, sir. Make the board—"

"Make the board what?" I cut in, my voice low and lethal. "See him as human? They don't care if he screws women on yachts. They care if he screws the balance sheet. And today, you let him walk out looking stronger than ever."

The man swallowed, his Adam's apple bobbing. "I—I paid the private investigator myself. He said it would destabilize him—"

"Destabilize?" I laughed, sharp and humorless. "He turned it into leverage. Into sympathy." My fist slammed against the desk, rattling the glasses. "Do better."

The second staffer, a younger woman with clipped speech and sharper eyes, stepped forward cautiously. "There… may be another angle."

I looked up. "Talk."

She slid a folder across the desk. Not glossy photos this time, but typed notes, lines of connections, whispers pulled from shadows. "I called on some sources to look into Noelle Collins. Clients think she came from nothing, built her empire from grit. The perfect rags-to-riches story. But if you dig far enough into her background, there's a brother. Not the kind you parade at galas."

My pulse quickened. "Go on."

"Black market art," she said simply. "High-value dealings. Untraceable transactions. He's kept himself clean in public, but people in the right circles know. And if we tie her success to him — seed money, influence, whatever story we craft — suddenly she's not self-made. She's a fraud."

The room went quiet except for the thrum of my pulse.

That was it. The crack. The opening.

I leaned back slowly, letting the idea settle, savoring it like the first sip of good whiskey. "And if she's a fraud," I said softly, "then Ezra isn't loyal. He's careless. Reckless. Endangering the family and the company with a woman who'll drag us all into scandal."

The woman nodded once, "Exactly, sir."

The third staffer shifted nervously. "It's… risky. If it backfires?"

"We make sure it doesn't," I cut him off. My voice was smooth again, controlled, but the rage simmered beneath it. "Find proof. Real proof. I don't care how buried it is. I want every whisper, every transaction, every rumor tied to that brother. And I want it yesterday."

The first staffer hesitated. "And if there isn't proof?"

I smiled then — slow, sharp, predatory. "Then we build it."

The silence after that was absolute. None of them dared speak. The only sound was the crunch of glass under my shoes as I stepped over the shattered crest.

Ezra thought he'd won today. Let him.

Very soon, I'd take everything from him — starting with the woman he thought he could protect.

***

Vivienne

Passing by his office I saw and heard Malcolm berating his staff Raised, sharp. Malcolm's tone — clipped with rage — and the smaller, tremulous responses of staff trying to keep up.

I should've kept walking. I should've headed straight down the corridor, slipped into my corner office, and pretended not to hear. But something in his voice made me pause — a jagged edge I hadn't heard before in our five years of knowing each other.

I lingered just beyond the threshold, back pressed to the cool paneled wall, heart thrumming too fast.

"… yacht photos weren't enough," Malcolm snarled. "He turned it into leverage. Into sympathy."

My pulse spiked. Ezra. Always Ezra.

I leaned closer, careful with my breath, straining to catch the rest.

"Another angle," a woman's voice. Calm, clinical. "Noelle Collins. On paper, she's self-made. But if you dig, there's family. A brother. Black market art. Discreet, but known in the right circles."

The words chilled me, each syllable tightening around my ribs.

Malcolm's laugh was low, cold. "That's it. That's the crack. Paint her as a fraud, Ezra as reckless. He doesn't just endanger himself — he endangers us all."

The silence that followed was heavy enough to choke on. And then his voice again, quieter now, colder: "Find proof. And if there isn't any? We'll build it."

A chair scraped. The muffled sound of papers shifting. And then nothing.

I stood frozen, nails digging crescents into my palms.

Black market art. A brother. Noelle Collins.

The names threaded into something dangerous, something that would tear through Ezra first, then ripple outward until the whole family was caught in the undertow.

I drew back before anyone emerged, heels silent against the carpet as I retreated down the hall. My chest was tight, my mind racing.

Tell Ezra. That was the first thought. He deserved to know what Malcolm was plotting, what kind of storm was being manufactured around him. He deserved more than this endless war disguised as family loyalty.

But the second thought… it was colder. More practical.

If I warned Ezra, I'd be betraying Malcolm. And no one betrayed Malcolm lightly. He remembered slights the way Evelyn remembered birthdays — perfectly, forever. Aligning myself against him could cost me more than my position at this table.

Husband or brother.

The choice lodged like glass in my throat. Ezra, who had stood reliably at my side, even when the family treated me like a convenient ornament. Who deserved peace, even if he'd never admit needing it. Or Malcolm, the husband whose temper burned as much for me as against me.

My reflection stared back in the elevator's mirrored doors as they slid shut, expression betraying nothing.

But inside, my stomach coiled.

Because whichever way I leaned, blood would spill.

CHAPTER 32

The Weight and the Warmth

Noelle

For the first time in weeks, my chest didn't feel like it was collapsing inward. Ezra's hand in mine, the way his voice had caught when he said the words I'd never let myself imagine — it left me unsteady, breathless, alive.

But under that warmth, something colder coiled. Cost. That word wouldn't leave me alone. What it might cost him. What it might cost me. What it might cost the life I'd sanded smooth and polished until it gleamed.

I curled into the corner of my couch, the city lit up behind glass, my phone burning in my palm. My thumb hovered over a name I hadn't pressed in years. Not because I'd forgotten him. But because I already worried about him too much, and I couldn't bear the thought of him turning that worry back on me. He'd always been quick to anger, quick to defend — a fire that burned hot and fast.

Still, I pressed.

"Nellie."

The word wrapped around me like smoke, low and dry, the same voice that used to whisper across bunk beds and back porches when we were kids. Hearing it now cracked something open — how close we'd been, how close I wished we still were. How much I missed him.

"Hey Cal," I said softly.

Silence first. Then a short laugh, humorless. "Guess you remembered my number."

"I guess that's fair." I tried for lightness, but the words faltered. "I just… couldn't."

He let the quiet stretch until it hurt. Then: "Something's wrong. Tell me."

My breath trembled. "I've lived with attention for years — articles, interviews, people calling me the "tri-coastal matchmaker," I swallowed hard. "That kind of spotlight, I could control. But now? Now it feels different. Heavier. Like there are eyes on me that don't blink. Questions coming from places that never used to care."

"Why now?" His tone was sharp, cutting through hesitation the way it always had.

"Because I gave them a reason," I whispered. "I've been seeing Ezra Sinclair. CEO of Sinclair Holdings."

The silence that followed was colder than any winter.

"Sinclair," he repeated flatly. "So you walked into the lion's den."

"It wasn't about power. It just… happened. But the moment it went public, it changed everything. Powerful people don't just gossip. They investigate. They peel back layers until they find something to use." My throat tightened. "And if they find you—"

"They won't." His voice was clipped, certain.

"You can't know that."

"I can." The edge in his tone sharpened. "Loose ends are tied. Cleaner than anyone gives me credit for. I don't play sloppy, Nellie. Not then, not now."

Hearing him call me Nellie again pulled a thread deep in my chest. It used to mean warmth, mischief, belonging. Now it reminded me how far we'd drifted, and how badly I wanted that closeness back.

"But the whispers—"

"Whispers don't build empires," he cut in. "Whispers don't put roofs over our heads. You built yours, I built mine.

Every gallery, every canvas, it's clean now. Clean enough for a spotlight, clean enough for an audit, clean enough for the Pope himself."

A shaky laugh escaped, caught between disbelief and relief. "You always could make me believe it."

"I don't sell to you," he said, voice softening. "I give you the truth. Don't let my name be the stone they throw at you. You earned what you have. Don't let them twist it."

"But if they push hard enough—"

"Then let them choke on it." His reply cracked like a whip, then steadied. "I've lived with shadows my whole life. I know how to carry them. You? For once, stop running from what you want."

The words hit too close. My throat ached.

"Promise me," I whispered, fragile as glass.

"I don't make promises." He paused. "But I don't break them either."

The line went quiet except for his breathing. And in that silence, I remembered what it meant to be a Collins — raised to walk the edge between survival and exposure, always braced for the blade.

"I love you," I said, barely audible.

"I know." His voice dropped lower, almost tender. "Now stop worrying about me. Enjoy what's yours, Nellie. Before they try to take it."

The call clicked off, leaving me alone with the city lights and the ache of a bond I wanted back, tighter now than before.

***

Nights like this, my townhouse felt too big. Too much glass, too much quiet, like it was holding its breath. After I hung up with my brother, the silence pressed on me even harder, and I needed something to do before I went out of my mind.

I drifted into the kitchen and just stood there for a second, staring at those copper pans I almost never touched. My life was always go-go-go — clients, flights, events. Takeout was my best friend. But tonight I wanted to cook. Not because I was hungry, but because I needed something simple, something real, something that felt like mine.

My phone sat on the counter, screen glowing. Ezra's name was right there. I scrolled past it twice before I gave in and tapped.

Come over?

The second I hit send, my phone buzzed back.

How long?

I hesitated, then typed: *An hour.*

Which was ridiculous, because an hour suddenly felt like five minutes.

The townhouse felt like it shifted the second I told him an hour. Suddenly every corner seemed to demand attention. I rushed through the kitchen, steak searing, potatoes roasting, asparagus tossed on a tray. Butter, garlic, rosemary crackled in the pan, filling the air while I darted back and forth — cooking, setting the table, running to the bedroom to swipe on mascara and pull on a dress that looked effortless, even though nothing about me in that moment was effortless.

By the time the knock came, the sauce was done, the oven timer was ticking down, and I was barefoot with an apron tied crooked at my waist, hair slipping loose from the pins I'd twisted in.

I opened the door, and there he was. Ezra leaned against the frame like he had all the time in the world, jeans and a soft T-shirt, his grin spreading slow as his eyes swept over me.

"You gonna invite me in," he said, voice low and playful, "or leave me out here pretending I don't smell steak?"

A laugh broke out of me before I could catch it, shaky and warm. "Come in before it burns."

He stepped past me, and the scent of his cologne folded into garlic and butter until the whole room felt like it belonged to us. His gaze moved over everything — the books stacked on the shelves, the quilt folded on the couch, the photo of my parents by the lamp.

"You cook, you decorate," he teased, that grin tugging at his mouth. "What can't you do?"

I shook my head, smiling despite myself.

Then his voice softened, more serious. "It's good to finally see your home. It looks like you. Feels like you."

I smiled and busied myself with the plates, setting them down more carefully than necessary. "How do you know what feels like me?"

He stepped closer, his hand brushing mine when I reached for the silverware. The touch lingered, sparking through me.

"Noelle," he said, deep and low. "You really want me to answer that?"

The timer went off, breaking the spell, and I pulled away to plate the food. We sat down at the table with two steaks, potatoes, asparagus, and a bottle of wine I'd been saving for nothing in particular.

Conversation flowed easier than I expected. He told me about Julian's antics, making me laugh so hard I had to cover my mouth with my napkin. I told him about my brother — careful with the shadows, but open with the love.

At one point, Ezra's laughter filled the room, deep and unguarded, and it hit me how much it changed the space. My townhouse had always felt sleek and quiet, but with him here, it felt alive. It felt like home.

When the plates were empty and the wine had dipped low, the chatter eased into silence. Not uncomfortable but heavier, like we both felt the same pull.

Ezra reached across the table, his fingers brushing mine — this time done in a way that there was no chance of pretending it was an accident.

"I could get used to this," he said, his eyes locked on me.

My chest warmed. "You sure about that?"

His grin softened, the usual edge gone. "I wouldn't be here if I didn't."

The words lingered between us, warm and terrifying all at once. For the first time, I didn't push them away. I let them stay. I let myself stay. And all I could think was: *what comes next?*

CHAPTER 33

Ezra

The night stayed with me as I left her place — garlic and butter still clinging to my shirt, her laugh echoing in my head, the quilt on her couch, the photo of her mother smiling through chemo. All those small, unpolished pieces of her life that most people would never see.

I'd wanted to pull her close, carry it further, but that wasn't what tonight was for. Tonight was about something else — showing her that I was there for *her*, not just the heat between us. And walking away with that truth settled deeper than anything else could.

The driver merged onto Allen Parkway, city lights streaking across the windshield. My phone buzzed. For a second, I thought it was her — that she'd wanted to hear my voice before sleep, or that she hadn't been able to stop thinking about me either.

It wasn't her.

Vivienne: *We need to talk. Post Oak Hotel bar. Tonight.*

My grip tightened around the phone. Vivienne didn't send bare messages like that. She filled them with emojis, exclamation marks, little flourishes to soften the edges. Four sharp words, a place, and a deadline meant only one thing: trouble.

I texted back. *On my way.*

The rest of the ride stretched tight. What could this be about? What could she be willing to risk pulling me aside for, away from the house, away from Malcolm's eyes? My sister didn't rattle easy. And she never picked a setting like the Post Oak unless she wanted privacy. That alone was enough to set my pulse climbing.

When I walked into the bar, it was as she intended — quiet, intimate, the kind of place where conversations disappeared into dark wood and low jazz. She was already waiting at a high-top, posture perfect, a glass of Chardonnay untouched in front of her. Vivienne never drank white wine. It was for show.

"Ezra." Her voice was calm, but her eyes flicked to the door before locking back on me. "Thanks for coming."

I sat across from her, unbuttoned my jacket, let the silence draw until she broke it.

"I couldn't do this at any of the houses," she said quickly, her hand twitching against the stem of her glass. "Malcolm would've noticed. He always notices."

The knot in my chest pulled tighter. "Then tell me."

Her voice dropped. "I overheard him. He was furious. Throwing things. Talking about how those yacht photos didn't land the way he wanted. And then one of his people said they had something better. Not about you. About her."

My jaw locked. "Noelle."

Vivienne nodded. "Her brother. They said he's not who people think he is. That if they had to, they'd investigate until they found something they could use. Ezra, he's circling her. If he finds anything — if he drags it out — it won't just hurt her. It'll burn you too."

The words hit hard. I leaned in, my voice low. "Why are you telling me this?"

She hesitated, then lifted her chin. "Because you're my brother. And because I saw the way you looked at her at the gala. You've never looked at anyone like that. Not Alexandra. Not anyone."

The noise of the bar faded. Only her words remained, sharp and undeniable.

"I don't want to see you destroyed," she went on, her voice breaking softer now. "But more than that, I don't want to see *her* destroyed. And Malcolm—he doesn't care who he cuts down as long as he wins."

My hand curled into a fist against the table. "Then I'll make sure he never gets the chance. I am going to go talk to Dad."

Her eyes searched mine, heavy with worry. "Be careful, Ezra. This isn't just business anymore."

I stood, the weight of it already set in me. "No," I said, my voice rough. "It never was."

***

The study smelled of leather and old wood, the kind of room built for legacies. My father sat behind the desk he'd claimed for three decades, his tie loosened, the lamplight cutting deep lines across his face. This wasn't the powerful man the city bowed to at galas. This was the version stripped back: tired, relentless, unbending.

"Close the door," he said.

I did. The click echoed like a gavel.

"You've made a mess, Ezra." His voice didn't rise, but it sliced all the same. "Rumors. Photographs with different women. I thought you were taking things with Alexandra serious, now you're with someone else. Investors wondering if you're too busy being a playboy to be taken seriously. "Tell me, what do you intend to do with this Collins girl?"

The name landed heavy between us.

I steadied my breath. "Mom already knows. I told her I want to handle it on my own and I'm telling you the same."

His eyes narrowed, sharp and assessing. "And are you even sure about her? She doesn't come from power. No family connections, no armor to shield you when the knives come out. There will be no merger of legacies here. So I'll ask you plain — is she worth it?"

The question cut deeper than the accusations. It wasn't about Noelle's worth; it was about whether I could carry mine without the scaffolding of another dynasty.

"I'm not you," I said finally, my voice even.

His gaze sharpened, warning. "Tread lightly, son."

"No," I pressed, my jaw locked. "I've spent my entire life being careful. Careful not to disappoint you. Careful not to tarnish the name. Careful to play the part. But careful isn't living. And it sure as hell isn't love."

The silence that followed was heavy, stretching across the desk like another shadow. For a moment I thought I'd crossed a line that couldn't be mended. Then his shoulders eased just slightly, and he leaned back in his chair.

"You think I wanted this?" His voice had dropped, quieter now, almost foreign. "This company. This chair. Do you think, at your age, I dreamed of balance sheets and endless meetings?"

I frowned. "You built this empire."

"No. I inherited a war." His eyes fixed on mine, hard and unflinching. "I was my father's only son. When he died, your uncle didn't even wait for the body to be cold before trying to rip this company from me. One hand in the coffin, the other in the vault. I buried my father, and before the dirt settled, I was already fighting to keep us from ruin."

He pushed back from the desk, stood, and crossed to the sideboard where decanters gleamed amber in the lamplight. His hands were slightly shaking as he poured two glasses of scotch. He slid one across the desk toward me. I didn't move to take it.

"Grief had to wait," he said, his voice tightening. "I didn't have time to mourn. I had to win. And the only reason I did — the only reason we still sit here with the Sinclair name intact — is because Evelyn steadied me. She kept everything moving when I wanted to break. She made sure the walls never showed cracks. That's how it began: an arrangement. But over time…"

His throat worked once. "She became the woman I love and whom I'd go to the ends of the earth for. That's what kept me alive when my own blood turned on me."

I studied him in the dim light — not the patriarch, but the man underneath. A man who'd been forced into battles he never chose. A man who'd built love out of survival.

"You and I aren't the same," he said after a moment, his voice firm again. "Maybe that unsettles me most. You actually want the work. You care in a way I never did. Which means you may not need what I needed."

Noelle's laugh flashed through my mind, the curve of her shoulder against me, the way her fire had felt like freedom.

He set his glass down, the crystal clink sharp in the quiet. "But don't mistake that for approval. I don't see what she brings to the table yet. She's untested. She doesn't carry the armor you'll need when this family is attacked again."

My fists clenched at my sides. "Then I'll make you see it."

Something flickered across his face. Not warmth — he didn't give warmth freely. But recognition. The faintest tug at the corner of his mouth, like he'd caught a glimpse of himself in me whether he wanted to or not.

"Then fight for it, Ezra. The way I fought when my brother came for this company. If she's worth it, prove it. To me. To everyone."

He dropped back into his chair, picked up his pen, and bent over his papers, signaling the conversation was finished.

But for the first time in my life, I didn't feel dismissed.

I felt challenged.

And I intended to rise to it.

CHAPTER 34

The Debut

Noelle

Valeria's eyes shimmered like she was trying to keep from bursting. She sat perched on the edge of the chair across from me, twisting the diamond ring on her finger, the stone catching every bit of afternoon light that spilled through the blinds.

"I'm engaged," she whispered, and then the words broke into a laugh, full and breathless.

Warmth spread through my chest, catching me off guard. "Engaged? Valeria, that's—" My voice cracked with the smile tugging at it. "That's incredible. Congratulations."

She nodded, almost in disbelief at her own happiness. "I know it's fast, maybe too fast, but… when you know, you know. I didn't even realize how much I'd been holding back until now. He's everything I didn't know I needed."

Her eyes grew wet, and before I could blink, she was leaning across the desk, taking my hands in both of hers. "And it's because of you."

The words hit deeper than I expected. "It was my pleasure to be your matchmaker."

She squeezed my fingers, urgent and certain. "Noelle, you pushed me to see myself differently. You gave me something I didn't believe I deserved." Her breath hitched, then steadied. "You gave me love. That's not just business. That's a gift."

I swallowed hard, blinking back a sting. I do what I do for moments like this when a person realizes they've stepped into more than they dreamed possible.

"And I want you to be part of it," Valeria added suddenly, pulling her hands back only to clasp them tight in her lap. "I want you as a bridesmaid."

The pen slid uselessly across my notes. "Valeria… I couldn't. That wouldn't be professional. I'm your matchmaker, not—"

"Noelle." Valeria's tone was tender but firm, the way clients sometimes startled me most. "Treat it like a passion project. Treat it like what it really is. You gave me this happiness. Don't tell me you can't stand with me while I celebrate it."

I exhaled slowly, the weight of her sincerity disarming me. Finally, I nodded. "All right. Then it would be my honor."

Her smile lit up the room, and for a moment the air itself seemed to glow with it.

A knock tapped at the door. Sadie poked her head in. "Mr. Sinclair is here."

Valeria rose with a quick hug, her perfume light and warm. "Go on. Don't keep him waiting." She grinned, conspiratorial. "And thank you, Noelle. For everything."

She swept out, leaving the space quieter but still humming with her joy.

Then he walked in.

His presence cut through the silence, but it wasn't the reserved man I'd first met. He came straight to me, and pulled me into his arms before I could think to move.

"You look beautiful," he said against my hair, his voice low and rough with something that wasn't practiced.

My cheeks heated before I could stop them. "Thank you. You look… incredibly handsome today."

He drew back just enough to meet my eyes, and the look he gave me was like he was truly happy to see me. A man who had stopped pretending long ago, at least with me.

"I have something to ask you," he said, anticipation sparking beneath his calm.

I tilted my head, heart already pounding. "Go on."

"Our annual Sinclair Foundation Gala is coming up." He let the words settle, then added, "And I want you there. With me. As my date."

The air seemed to still around us. I'd been to events before, standing behind clients, orchestrating introductions, keeping my own life invisible. But this wasn't that. This was Ezra asking me to step into the center with him.

"Ezra…" My voice faltered. "That gala—it's not just a dinner. It's public. It's us out loud."

"That's exactly what I want," he said simply. His gaze didn't waver. "I don't want to keep this quiet anymore, Noelle. I want people to know who you are to me."

My chest tightened, not with doubt, but with the weight of the step itself. My throat worked before I whispered, "We've never actually said it out loud. What this is."

For the first time since I'd known him, his composure flickered. His jaw tightened. His fingers drummed once against his thigh before stilling. "Then let me say it." His voice was quieter now, rawer. "I see this as a relationship. If that's what you want too."

My heart slammed once, hard. He was waiting—Ezra Sinclair, the man who never bowed, never bent—waiting nervously for my answer.

I let the silence stretch, feeling the enormity of it, before I nodded slowly. "That's what I want too."

Relief crashed across his face, subtle but unmistakable, before a smile broke loose.

"Then come with me," he said softly, not as an order but as a plea. "Be mine—out loud."

I didn't answer yet, not fully. But the truth was already inside me, undeniable.

***

The townhouse was too quiet when I walked in. I kicked off my heels at the door, set my purse on the console, and stood in the stillness for a moment, letting the silence wrap around me. Normally, it felt like sanctuary after a long day. Tonight, it felt like judgment.

I should have canceled his contract the moment I realized. That was the professional thing, the safe thing. When the first flicker of attraction caught me off guard, I should've stepped back and drawn a line that couldn't blur.

But I hadn't until things got messy.

I drifted into the living room, glass of wine in hand, and my eyes found the wall. Dozens of framed photographs stretched across it—clients I had matched who'd gone on to stand under arches of flowers, to cut cakes with trembling hands, to dance with rings newly heavy on their fingers. Couples who had written to me afterward with words like *forever* and *because of you.*

Mr. Callahan's voice echoed in my memory, sure and certain: *My whole world.* He hadn't spoken it with regret. He'd spoken it with reverence. And I remembered the way it had pierced me—that hunger to want the same. Not fleeting sparks, not polished façades, but devotion that endured.

I traced a fingertip along one of the frames, the edges smooth from years of dusting. They had trusted me to lead them toward something real. How could I sit here, hiding from my own?

Fear tugged at me, whispering about appearances, about how much easier it had been to glide into galas as the matchmaker rather than step into the spotlight as someone's date. As *his* date.

But I wasn't that woman anymore.

Because it wasn't a question of whether I'd go.
It was whether I was ready for the world to see the way I already loved him.

I wanted to live fully. To stop shrinking myself to fit into roles that looked respectable, but left me empty. And with Ezra, I couldn't pretend anymore. He unsettled me, challenged me, saw me—not as the orchestrator behind the curtain, but as a woman. *His* woman.

My hand tightened around the phone. The gala would be intimidating, yes. Walking in beside him would be a storm I couldn't control. But wasn't that what I told my clients every day? That love wasn't found in control, but in the risk of letting yourself be seen?

I lifted the phone, thumb hovering before pressing his name. The line rang once. Twice.

Then his voice came, low and warm. "Collins."

I exhaled, a smile tugging despite the nerves coiled tight in my chest. "Ezra. About the gala…"

His silence sharpened, waiting.

I swallowed once, "Yes. I'll go with you."

***

The envelope was thick, heavy with promise, Ezra's handwriting scrawled across the front: *For whatever makes you feel unstoppable.* Inside, crisp bills—far too many for a single gown. My first instinct was to shove it back in his hands, to remind him I'd built my business without anyone's money but my own.

But the truth was, it wasn't about the money. It was about him saying, *don't hold back, I've got you.* About him wanting me to walk into that gala with every ounce of power I had.

So I called Shayla.

By noon the next day, we were in a boutique that smelled of new fabric and expensive perfume, surrounded by racks of gowns that glittered like galaxies under soft golden light. Shayla was already in her element, plucking sequins and silk like a personal stylist on commission.

"Try this one. And this one. And ooooh, this one will make him combust."

"Combust?" I deadpanned, clutching the pile of gowns.

She winked. "Explode. Ignite. Lose the ability to form words. Pick whichever fire metaphor makes you happiest."

I laughed, nerves dissolving as she shoved me toward the fitting rooms.

The first gown was too fussy, the second too matronly, the third so glittery I looked like a walking disco ball. But the fourth—

Black. Clean lines that skimmed my waist, a slit running high enough to make Shayla gasp. The neckline wasn't immodest, but it was daring, a frame that drew the eye like an invitation. The fabric moved when I walked—liquid, sensuous, like I'd been poured into midnight.

When I stepped out, Shayla slapped both hands over her mouth. Then she let out a shriek that made two sales associates peek over from across the boutique.

"Girl. GIRL." She spun me toward the mirror. "You look like you just descended from Mount Olympus. Beyoncé could *never.*"

I burst out laughing, shaking my head. "You're ridiculous."

"And you're a goddess," she shot back, tugging at the hem so the slit showed a little more leg. "Ezra Sinclair's going to forget his name when he sees you."

I arched a brow at my reflection. The woman staring back at me wasn't the careful, composed matchmaker the press had photographed at other galas. She was unapologetic. Powerful. Alive.

We found shoes to match—strappy stilettos that glittered like champagne in the light—and earrings that caught with every turn of my head. By the time we left, our arms were full of bags and our cheeks sore from laughing.

And Ezra still wasn't finished.

That evening, a discreet knock at my door brought a team of stylists he'd sent: hair, makeup, nails. My living room transformed into a beauty lounge in under ten minutes, Shayla perched with a glass of prosecco while someone coaxed her curls into a crown of glossy waves.

"Why do I feel like I'm in a rom-com montage?" she muttered, grinning as a nail tech filed her hand.

"Because you are," I teased, though my heart was pounding when the stylist swept a final curl into place and dusted shimmer over my shoulders.

By the time they were finished, I barely recognized myself. My hair framed my face in soft, polished waves; my eyes smoldered beneath lashes I hadn't known could curl that high. My lips gleamed in a rose shade that whispered more than it shouted. For the first time in a long time, I felt… luminous.

Another knock broke the hum of blow dryers and chatter. This time, Shayla's husband, Marcus, stepped in. Tall, broad-shouldered, fitted tux hugging him like it was tailored hours ago. He smelled of sandalwood and fresh cologne, and when he smiled at Shayla, the whole room softened.

"Well damn," Shayla muttered, fanning herself theatrically. "How did I get so lucky?"

I grinned, but the truth was, seeing them together sent a quiet ache through me. The way his hand automatically found her waist, how she leaned into him without thinking—it was ease, history, devotion. The kind of love that looked lived-in and unshakable.

"Ezra invited us, right?" Marcus asked, scanning the room with a chuckle. "For moral support?"

"Exactly," Shayla said, kissing his cheek. "Noelle's got the date of the year, and we're not letting her walk into that lion's den without backup."

When Ezra finally arrived, he didn't knock politely. He walked in like the space already belonged to him—then stopped.

His gaze dragged over me, slow, like he was memorizing every detail. From the curve of the gown's neckline to the glint of my heels, down to the slit that revealed just enough leg to tempt him further. His jaw worked once before he finally found words.

"We don't really have to go anywhere," he said, voice low and rough. "Not when you look like *that*."

Shayla, ever the instigator, snorted into her prosecco. "Told you he'd combust."

I rolled my eyes, though warmth crept up my neck. "Nice try, Sinclair. But we're going to this gala."

He stepped closer, his cologne wrapping around me—cedar and citrus, crisp and commanding. "Are you sure? Because I could spend the rest of the night right here… convincing you otherwise."

I pressed a hand to his chest, steadying the thrum of my own pulse. His heartbeat was solid and strong beneath my palm, "Tempting. But tonight, you don't get to keep me to yourself. Tonight, you get to show me off."

A slow and wolfish grin began to spread across his face. His eyes darkened, unreadable but charged. "Careful. I might get used to that."

I tilted my chin. "Maybe I want you to."

Shayla groaned, grabbing her clutch. "Lord, y'all are *disgusting*. And hot. Mostly hot. But still disgusting."

Ezra's grin widened as he offered me his arm, polished and old-world. "Shall we, Ms. Collins?"

I slid my hand into the crook of his elbow, pulse racing. Marcus stepped up beside Shayla, her hand sliding naturally into his.

And for one breathtaking second, as the four of us headed out, I realized: this wasn't just about survival or appearances anymore. This was about walking into the world with him at my side—and choosing it.

The black-carpet stretched long beneath the glittering awning of the hotel, camera flashes already firing like fireworks. When Ezra offered his arm, I slid my hand into place, heart pounding. The double doors swung open, and the room seemed to hush as we stepped inside.

All eyes turned.

Crystal chandeliers dripped light across marble floors and gilded pillars. Waiters in white jackets wove through the crowd with champagne flutes. A string quartet played from the mezzanine, their music cutting smooth and sharp through the hum of conversation.

And every head swiveled toward us. Toward *him*. Toward *me*.

Ezra's hand settled lightly at my back, like an anchor as he guided me deeper into the room. "You're stunning," he murmured against my ear, his tone low enough for me alone.

"Good," I whispered back, lips curving. "Because they're staring."

"Let them."

He introduced me with calm precision—investors, socialites, the city's mayor, each greeted with warmth sharpened by his unshakable poise.

And then Evelyn herself glided forward, silk and diamonds, her smile polished enough to blind. Cameras shifted instantly, snapping as she took both my hands in hers.

"Noelle," she said warmly, though the pause between syllables was sharp. "The last time we spoke, you were Ezra's matchmaker. And now—his date. How… poetic."

Her cheek brushed mine, her perfume expensive. I held my smile, the warmth of Ezra's palm on my back grounding me. He leaned in, low enough for only me to hear: "Breathe. I've got you."

The flashbulbs caught us together, Evelyn glowing at my side, Ezra tall and confident on the other. The optics were perfect. Almost too perfect.

Later, the speech. Ezra stood at the podium, the room stilled under his voice, strong and commanding. He spoke of legacy, of the foundation's work, of carrying forward something his father had built. And then—unexpectedly—his hand reached for mine, drawing me up beside him.

"This year is different," he said, gaze sweeping the crowd before settling on me. "Because this year, I don't stand here alone. Tonight, I stand here with the woman I love."

The words crashed through me, stealing breath, stealing everything. It was one thing to say it to each other and another to have it declared to the world, or the stage of this gala.

The room erupted—applause, gasps, the flash of cameras like lightning. But all I could hear was his voice, the conviction in it.

When he drew me close for a kiss at the edge of the stage, it wasn't just for show. It was real. Too real. My knees nearly gave.

Later, in the glow of it, Alexandra slithered close—sleek dress, sharper smile. "Well," she said, eyes flicking between us, "This is lasting longer than I thought." Her laugh was glass on glass before she swept away.

At dinner, Vivienne reached across the table, her hand brushing mine with genuine warmth. "I'm happy for you," she said softly. Julian raised his glass, grinning. "You've got a long way to go before you're worrying about weddings and kids. Don't let them saddle you with that yet."

Her husband, meanwhile, sipped his scotch like it owed him something, jaw tight, eyes too sharp.

The gala had settled into its rhythm—waiters gliding past with champagne, clusters of donors swapping stories, the string quartet soft in the background. Ezra bent toward me as another hand caught his arm. A senator, eager to talk strategy.

"Go ahead," I murmured, squeezing his hand. "I'll find Shayla."

His eyes lingered, reluctant, before he nodded and moved toward the circle of power-brokers. I slipped through the crowd, scanning for Shayla's gown.

That's when a man I didn't recognize stepped into my path, a drink already in his hand. His smile was too slick, his eyes too sharp.

"You shouldn't be standing here by yourself," he said smoothly, leaning in just enough to make me bristle. "A woman like you deserves attention."

I shifted back a step, keeping my voice polite but firm. "Thank you. But I'm not interested."

He chuckled like I'd told a joke. "Everyone's interested, eventually."

My pulse ticked higher. Before I could retort, Shayla appeared at my side, brows lifted. "She said she's not interested." Her tone carried the warning only another woman could give.

The man's smirk soured. "Relax. Just being friendly." But his body edged closer, the reek of liquor rolling off him.

"Back up," Shayla snapped, shifting subtly between us.

He scoffed, rolling his eyes. "What is this, a chaperone?"

And then Ezra was there. He didn't raise his voice. He didn't need to.

"She said no."

The weight in his tone froze the air, low and lethal. He stepped in, one hand pressing firmly against the man's chest, forcing him back. "You're done."

Security moved fast, summoned with a flick of Ezra's hand. The man sputtered protests, but two guards closed in, escorting him toward the doors.

I exhaled, only realizing then how tightly I'd been holding my breath. Shayla touched my arm, lightly and protective.

Ezra turned to me, eyes searching, jaw still taut. "You all right?"

I nodded, though my pulse was still racing. His hand brushed my waist, grounding me, the storm in him barely leashed as he leaned closer.

"No one touches what's mine," he said quietly—more to me than anyone else—before straightening again.

The room never fully quieted, but I felt the shift— conversations softer, eyes lingering, the sense of an audience waiting for what came next. Ezra's attention never wavered. It was fixed on me, unrelenting, as if none of them existed.

The orchestra struck its cue, violins rising, a current carrying couples toward the floor. Space opened in the center, chandeliers casting wide arcs of gold across the polished wood. Ezra extended his hand. He didn't ask. He simply offered.

I placed my hand in his.

He drew me in until I fit against him, one hand at my waist, the other folding firmly around mine. His steps were sure, practiced, pulling me into the rhythm with ease. Around us, gowns swept, heels slid, laughter carried—but he anchored me, his gaze holding me in place.

"This isn't for them," he said, his voice low, meant only for me. "This is for us."

"I love you, Ezra."

He slowed just enough that I felt the weight of it land. His jaw shifted, the line of his mouth easing, his eyes deepening into something unguarded. He bent closer, his forehead brushing mine, his breath warm between us.

"Say it again."

"I love you."

The room blurred. Maybe people were whispering. Maybe flashes sparked in the background. All I knew was the pull between us, the quiet recognition that this moment wasn't a performance. It was truth.

The music softened, the dance slowing, but he didn't release me. My cheek rested against the crisp line of his jacket, the faint scent of cedar clinging to him. I spoke into the space between us. "I want you to meet my family. The man who matters most to me… needs to meet the most important people in my life."

His arm tightened, his reply immediate. "Tell me when. Tell me where. I'll be there."

Another song began, drawing couples closer together, but I hardly noticed. Ezra held me as if we had nowhere else to be.

And I understood—this wasn't Ezra Sinclair, heir to an empire. This was the man I loved. The man I'd chosen. And tonight, he had chosen me back, in full view of everyone watching.

***

The night ended at my townhouse.. Whiskey by the fire, laughter easing the sharp edges of the gala until the silence between us felt too loaded to ignore. When he kissed me, it was certain and slow, like he'd decided long ago that we would end here. Hours later, I fell asleep in sheets, the hum of his breath brushed against my skin.

Sun rays cut across the marble floor when I woke. Ezra stood in the doorway already dressed, shirt-sleeves rolled, coffee cup in hand. His gaze caught on me, softer than I'd ever seen it.

"Morning," he said, his voice low, scratchy.

I started to pull the sheet closer, but realized I felt more comfortable than I've ever been. "Morning."

He came into the kitchen with me, pouring me coffee like it was the most natural thing in the world. For a while, we just sipped in silence, the quiet almost domestic—dangerously easy.

But the words pressed at me until I couldn't swallow them anymore. I set my cup down, fingers lingering on the rim.

"Since we are now serious, there's something you should know."

His head lifted, all focus. "What's that?"

I hesitated, nerves knotting my stomach. "My brother has dealt with illegal art."

His expression didn't change immediately—too careful, too unreadable. My pulse jumped. "Okay."

The silence stretched, and I felt exposed, like I'd peeled back something I wasn't sure he wanted. "I know it's a lot," I rushed on. "You've got a whole world that runs on its own rules, and this—this is different. My family isn't…" I stopped myself. "I just need to know if that's something you want."

He set his cup down slowly, leaned closer over the counter, and studied me with that unflinching gaze. His hand came down over mine, warm and sure. "Hear me clearly. Okay. It changes nothing."

The relief hit sharp, almost dizzying—but so did the weight of it. Because this wasn't just a man saying yes to me. It was Ezra Sinclair embracing the most personal corners of my life.

And that terrified me almost as much as it thrilled me.

***

After a day spent with Ezra, he left and the townhouse returned to its usual quiet. The kind of quiet that didn't soothe but echoed. I slipped off my heels, lined them neatly by the door, and let my body sag against the wall. For the first time all night, I let the smile drop.

The gala had been… everything. The cameras, the eyes, the subtle weight of whispers—those I expected. What I hadn't expected was how it felt to walk in on Ezra's arm and not have to pretend anymore. To laugh too loud at something he said. To lean in when I should have leaned back. To feel, even for a few hours, like the city wasn't pressing in on us with its judgments.

But joy had edges. The whole time I kept waiting for the other shoe to drop—the photo, the whisper, the headline that would reduce me to an interloper again. It didn't come, not yet. Which only made the anticipation worse.

And then there was what I'd done. The invitation slipped out before I'd thought it through. *Sunday dinner.* My parents' table. My brother. The most unpolished, uncurated part of me. I hadn't asked, hadn't warned them. I could already hear my mother's careful pause, my father's skeptical eyebrow, the silence my brother carried like a second skin.

What would they say when Ezra Sinclair walked through the door? Would they see what I saw—that he was more than a billionaire playboy, more than the Sinclair heir? Or would they see only the danger, the storm already circling us?

I curled onto the sofa, tucking my knees against my chest, and stared at the ceiling until my eyes burned. Tonight had been both the happiest and the most precarious night of my life—walking openly beside the man I loved while every part of me braced for collapse.

And still, when I closed my eyes, all I felt was the warmth of his hand on mine, steady in the middle of the storm.

CHAPTER 35

Meet the Collins

Ezra

The car rolled to a stop in front of a modest brick house with a porch light glowing against the dusk. Not the kind of place guarded by gates and staff, but one that carried a different weight—the weight of family.

I wanted to know the people who'd raised Noelle. What I didn't want was for them to already think they knew me— based on a last name, a blog, or a rumor whispered in the right circles.

Noelle's hand brushed mine as I came around to open her door. She looked calm, but I knew her well enough by now to catch the flicker of nerves under the calm.

Her mother opened the door before we knocked. She kissed Noelle's cheek, then turned her eyes on me—polite, but sharp in a way that told me this was more than a courtesy greeting.

"Mrs. Collins," I said, extending my hand. "Thank you for having me."

Her smile was faint, measured. "Come in."

The smell of cornbread and greens carried through the house, warm and grounding. Her father rose from the table as we entered, his posture telling me this was no casual dinner.

Good. I respected a man who made his expectations plain.

The questions started as soon as we sat down. Noelle's father leaned forward, his tone skeptical but polite. "You've built a reputation for moving fast. Aggressive expansions, bold acquisitions. Tell me—do you ever stop to think about the cost? To the people under you, the ones who don't have the cushion your name gives you?"

I let the weight of it settle. He wasn't asking about numbers. He was asking about me.

"I think about it every day," I said evenly. "I've seen what happens when leaders forget the people who keep the lights on. My father taught me a business survives because of balance— vision, yes, but also loyalty. You take care of your people, they'll take care of the company. I'd put that against any market strategy."

His eyes narrowed slightly, searching for cracks.

Then her mother spoke, her voice soft but sharp. "That sounds polished. But what I want to know is whether you'll treat my daughter the same way. Will you take care of her, or is she just another part of your… acquisitions?"

Noelle shifted, ready to speak, but I reached for her hand beneath the table before she could. My voice stayed even.

"She's not part of anything," I said. "She's the point. I didn't come here to talk about Sinclair Holdings. I came because I wanted you to see that the man at this table isn't a headline or a name. He's someone who wants to build something real with your daughter. And for that to last, I know I'll need more than her trust. I'll need yours too."

The silence that followed pressed hard. Her father's gaze flicked to Noelle, then back to me. Her mother's expression softened, if only a fraction.

Noelle's hand tightened around mine, her eyes shining with quiet resolve.

For the first time that evening, I allowed myself a careful breath.

That was when the knock came at the door.

Before I could even shift in my seat, her mother was already standing, a smile tugging her mouth into something brighter than I'd seen all night. "That'll be him," she said, voice light.

Him?

She opened the door, and there was a man I assumed to be her brother.

Not a surprise. Not uninvited. They'd asked him here.

The atmosphere changed instantly. Where the house had been taut with wary silence, it bloomed with warmth at his arrival. Her father clapped him on the back like a prodigal son returning, her mother fussed about his weight, insisting he looked too thin, and Noelle—Noelle's whole face softened.

I saw her shoulders drop in relief when he kissed her cheek, like some invisible weight had shifted. She swatted at his hand when he reached for a biscuit from the counter, laughter spilling out of her as if no one else in the room mattered for a moment.

"Y'all really started without me?" he teased, sliding into the kitchen like he'd always belonged there. He stirred a pot, sampled a taste, nodded approvingly, then dropped a kiss on his mother's cheek again before she could scold him.

Her parents looked at him like he hung the moon. The sternness that had been aimed at me only minutes earlier was nowhere in sight. They glowed in his presence, proud, protective, and I couldn't miss the subtext—he was theirs in a way I might never be.

And he was good. Too good. Effortless. A man who could pull everyone into his orbit without breaking a sweat.

Which is why the unease dug deeper.

Because Noelle had been tense about this. She hadn't wanted him here, not like this, not tonight. And yet here he was—charming, attentive, warm. A brother who seemed like he'd do anything for his family.

What was I missing?

I watched her watch him, caught the flicker in her eyes when his jokes rolled too easily off his tongue. To anyone else it was sibling affection, years of closeness, shorthand built in the marrow. But there was something more in her glance. Something I couldn't name yet, except to know it was wrapped in fear.

Her parents were delighted. The room hummed now with easy chatter, the tension cut in half. But for me, the warmth was laced with questions that wouldn't let go.

If this man was her brother—why did she hide him? Why did his presence, so perfectly benign on the surface, feel like a risk she hadn't wanted to take?

And why, sitting at this table with her family gathered around him, did I feel like I'd just been handed the piece of the puzzle I wasn't supposed to see?

***

The house had settled into that hush that comes after a big meal. Dishes stacked in the sink, the scent of roasted meat and cornbread still heavy in the air. Noelle was in the kitchen with her mother, her laugh carrying low and warm as they packed leftovers into containers.

Then her father's hand settled on my shoulder. Firm. Heavy.

"Ezra," he said quietly. "Step outside with me."

It wasn't a suggestion.

He led me through the back door, out onto a wide porch that overlooked a narrow yard washed gold by the setting sun. Cicadas hummed loud in the trees, their endless song filling the space between us. He leaned against the railing, arms crossed, studying me like a man weighing whether land was worth the investment.

"My daughter doesn't bring men home," he began, voice measured but sharp at the edges. "Not for Sunday dinner. Not ever. So I have to assume you're serious."

"I am," I said, the words steady.

His gaze hardened. "Serious how? A fling can feel serious when it's new. What do you see when you look at her future? And do you see yourself in it?"

The question landed heavy, but I didn't flinch. "I see a woman who built something from the ground up when everyone said she couldn't. She's tougher than she lets on, smarter than anyone in the room gives her credit for. She deserves more than being used as a pawn in anyone's game— mine, yours, or anyone else's. And I want a future with her. Not because it looks good on paper, but because she makes me better than I am without her."

The screen door creaked, and her brother stepped out. He leaned against the opposite post, arms folded, eyes sharp as his father's but younger, more calculating.

"You talk good," he said, tone even. "But talk's cheap."

I turned toward him. "Then ask me what you need to know."

And he did. Question after question—about my family, about what happened with Alexandra, about what Noelle risked by being tied to me. Some questions stung more than others, but I answered each one without hedging, without running. Because this was the price of being with her, and I wasn't going anywhere.

When he finally fell quiet, he studied me for a long moment. Then he stepped closer, pulled a slim file from under his arm, and handed it over.

"Read it," he said. "Then decide what you're going to do with it."

I flipped it open. My pulse jumped at the first page. Malcolm. Dates. Accounts. Transactions that weren't supposed to exist. Proof of things I'd only suspected, laid out in black and white.

By the time I shut the folder, my jaw was tight enough to ache.

"Why give this to me?" I asked.

"Because she trusts you," her brother said simply. "And if you're half the man you just claimed to be, you'll use it to protect her."

I nodded, sliding the file under my arm. He didn't need to know what I was already thinking—that before I made a single move with this, I had to talk to Vivienne. She'd warned me about Malcolm first. She deserved a warning in return, before I turned this into a war.

The cicadas screamed louder, the scent of cornbread drifting from inside. Noelle's laughter floated through the screen door, soft and unguarded, and it struck me all over again what I was fighting for.

Not the company. Not survival. Her.

And I intended to prove it—starting with this file in my hands.

The night hummed with summer air when we left my parents' house. Cicadas droned like static, and the scent of grilled meat still clung faintly to my dress. Ezra's hand brushed the small of my back as we walked to his car. The gesture was simple, polite even, but my body read it like a promise.

"You survived," I teased, though my voice was thinner than I wanted.

He angled a look at me, eyes sharp in the wash of the porch light. "Barely. Your father interrogated me harder than a Senate hearing."

I laughed, easing some of the tightness in my chest. "He doesn't scare easily. But you did well."

"I wasn't sure." His jaw flexed, then softened. "Your brother stole the show."

The way he said it made me pause. Like he was still puzzling out who my brother really was, beneath the warmth and easy charm. I looked away, toward the drive. "He always does."

We didn't speak much on the way home. The silence wasn't heavy—it vibrated, charged, full of things unsaid. Streetlights carved gold bars across Ezra's profile: the hard line of his jaw, the relaxed grip on the wheel, the pinky that kept brushing the edge of the console like it wanted to touch mine and didn't quite dare.

When we pulled up in front of my place, I didn't move. My keys sat heavy in my lap.

"Thank you," he said finally, voice quiet but threaded with something deeper. "For letting me be there tonight."

I swallowed, heat rising under my skin. "Don't thank me."

His brow furrowed. "Why not?"

"Because if you do…" My throat tightened. "I might ask you to stay."

The silence snapped taut. His gaze locked on mine, unreadable but unrelenting.

"Say it again," he murmured.

"Stay," I whispered.

I was already out of the car before my courage dissolved, fumbling for the keys at the door with hands that wouldn't steady. Ezra followed, his footsteps sure, his presence filling the narrow hall behind me.

Inside, the townhouse felt different—like it was holding its breath too. I dropped my clutch onto the table, the sound sharp in the stillness. When I turned, he was already closing the door, his eyes never leaving mine.

We didn't move at first. We just stood there, the space between us thick with the weight of every rule I'd broken by letting him this close. My heart hammered so loud I was sure he could hear it.

Then he was across the room, hands framing my face, mouth crushing against mine.

The kiss was fire and undoing. It wasn't gentle, wasn't measured—it was a month of restraint breaking open, raw and hungry. I clutched at his shirt, desperate for something solid as the world tilted. He pressed me back against the door, his body a wall of heat and intent, and for once I didn't care about the risk. I cared about him. About this.

When he broke away, his forehead pressed to mine, his breath ragged, his voice shook with restraint. "Are you sure?"

"Yes."

The word was small, but it cracked something wide open.

He kissed me again, slower this time, reverent. His hands slid down, anchoring me, but careful—always careful—as if he knew how easily I might shatter. I led him toward the bedroom, each step both terrifying and inevitable.

Inside, the city glowed faintly through the glass wall, bathing us in fractured light. My hands trembled as I reached for the buttons of his shirt, but his covered mine, steadying me.

"You don't have to rush," he murmured.

"I don't want to wait," I whispered back.

The rest blurred into heat and breath and the sound of my own heartbeat crashing in my ears. Clothes fell, touch replaced words, and somewhere between the urgency and the tenderness, the fear I'd carried for so long began to fade away.

When it was over, we lay tangled in the sheets, the air still charged with what we'd done. His arm wrapped around me, my head resting against his chest, our breaths finally syncing.

For the first time in years, I let myself feel small. Not weak—just… held.

His hand brushed up and down my arm absently, as if even in sleep he wouldn't let go.

And as my eyes fluttered shut, one truth anchored me in place: I'd crossed the line I swore I never would.

And I didn't regret it. Not tonight.

CHAPTER 36

House of Sinclair

Ezra

The last time I was in this study, I'd stumbled on Noelle hiding here after dinner, two champagne flutes perched on the table like she'd been deciding whether to celebrate or escape. I remember the muffled hum of conversation spilling down the hallway, the clink of cutlery from the dining room, and her shoulders tight until she realized it was me. That nervous smile—half-defiance, half-relief—still lingers in my head. We hadn't spoken in thirty-four days before that night. That was the first moment, the crack in the dam.

Standing here again, the air feels heavy with that memory. But now, we're not pretending anymore. Noelle isn't just the woman slipping away from the crowd; she's the woman I claim without apology. The thought steadies me even as I brace for what comes next.

The door opened, and Vivienne slipped inside. She closed it carefully, her back to the wood for a moment before turning. Her eyes found me, sharp and uncertain all at once.

"You said it couldn't wait," she murmured.

"It can't." I set the folder on the desk between us, the leather blotter catching its weight. Her gaze dropped, curious at first—then wary.

"Ezra…"

"Read it," I said quietly.

She hesitated, then flipped it open. Her face changed line by line—confusion first, then disbelief, then anger so raw it shook her hands. When she looked up again, her eyes were glassed, fury and hurt caught together.

"I should've known," she whispered. Her voice cracked. "If he's capable of scheming on everyone else, why would I be the exception?"

"Viv—"

She shook her head, pressing a trembling hand to her temple, closing the file as if the words inside could burn her. "Don't. I don't want to fall apart in front of you. Not yet." Her breath stuttered, and she forced her shoulders straight. "I'll hold it until the time comes. Until it matters. But God help me, Ezra, I will not let him be the one to destroy me."

I stood there, silent, watching my sister—polished, poised Vivienne—crack and rebuild herself in the span of seconds. The fire in her eyes was familiar. It was ours.

And in that moment, I knew: before I moved on this, I had to give her the same courtesy she'd given me. A warning. A chance to decide how she wanted her truth to land when it was finally exposed.

***

Noelle

The car wound up the long drive, that familiar, deliberate curve meant to impress more than welcome. The Sinclair house came into view—stone, glass, and symmetry gleaming in the twilight. My chest tightened as the iron gates closed behind us. No matter how many times I came here, the place always carried a weight. This wasn't just dinner. It never was.

His hand found mine before we approached the door. Firm. Warm. A quiet reminder.

"You're with me," he said.

I nodded, though my stomach was a storm. I'd faced clients sharper than knives, families who'd whispered about me before shaking my hand. But this—this was different. This was *his* family. The first time I was here, I was being honored for finding him a match, but now I am the match.

I tried to stand straighter, to remind myself I belonged, because he wanted me here. Still, I felt the scrutiny before I even saw her.

Evelyn Sinclair. Perfect posture, pearls at her throat, eyes that missed nothing.

"Noelle," she greeted smoothly, a smile just shy of warmth. "Welcome."

I offered mine in return, careful but sincere. "Thank you for having me."

Ezra's hand never left the small of my back as he led me inside, past the staff moving soundlessly, past Vivienne watching from the landing above. He was relaxed, the way he only seemed to be when it was just the two of us, and that steadiness bled into me.

The dining room gleamed with crystal and silver, every detail set like a stage. I took my seat beside him, aware of every eye in the room measuring me. The food arrived in courses, but I barely tasted it. What I did taste was Ezra's quiet defiance—how he poured my wine first, how he listened when I spoke, how he laughed low at something I whispered when the table grew too tense.

Evelyn Sinclair sat across from me, posture so flawless it could have cut glass. Her smile was soft, but her questions weren't.

"So, Noelle it's lovely to see you here again," she began, tone polite, eyes sharp. "Tell us—what exactly drew you into matchmaking? A rather… unconventional profession, isn't it?"

I swallowed, keeping my expression smooth. "I've always believed people deserve to be seen for who they are, not just what they can offer. Matchmaking gave me a way to build something on my own terms."

She tilted her head and stared at me with a hint of amusement, "And now here you are with Ezra. Remarkable, isn't it, how paths cross?"

Julian, seated two chairs down, leaned forward with a wide grin. "Remarkable and earned. Noelle's made a name for herself. That deserves respect."

"Respect," Malcolm drawled from the far end of the table, cutting into his steak like it had wronged him. "Or attention. Which is it, Ezra? Because we've all seen this before. Flavor of the month, gossip blog smiles, then the next one comes along." His gaze flicked to me, cruel and dismissive. "Who's after her?"

The words sliced through me before I could even process them. My fork stilled. My chest tightened.

And then I felt Ezra. The shift in him was immediate—his hand tightened over mine beneath the table, jaw locking, eyes narrowing in a way that pulled the air right out of the room. And then, before I could process what was happening, his chair scraped back against the floor.

The sound of Ezra's fist connecting with Malcolm's jaw cracked through the dining room like thunder. Gasps broke out—Evelyn's sharp inhale, Julian's half-formed protest—but I couldn't move. Malcolm stumbled back, clutching his face, his smirk gone, eyes burning with something uglier.

Ezra stood over him, chest heaving, voice low and lethal. "Don't ever fix your mouth to talk about her in that way again. If you do, I won't stop at one punch."

The table was stunned into silence. Even Evelyn didn't speak.

Ezra turned, his hand finding mine again, this time pulling me up with him. His touch wasn't gentle, but it wasn't reckless either—it was decisive. Protective. Final.

"We're leaving." His words weren't a request.

No one stopped us. Not Julian, not Evelyn. Not even Malcolm, who sat back down with blood at the corner of his mouth, glaring daggers as if he'd been waiting for this moment all along.

Ezra didn't slow until the heavy doors of the estate closed behind us. His driver was waiting, door open. He ushered me inside without a word, then slid in next to me, still radiating fury.

The silence in the car was sharp, the kind that leaves no room for doubt. Finally, Ezra spoke, his voice low and unshakable.
"We're going to my house."

And for the first time all night, the knot in my chest loosened. Not because the tension was gone, but because Ezra had made his choice clear—in front of everyone.

***

Ezra

The gray wash of dawn crept through the tall windows of my bedroom, softening the sharp lines of the city outside. Noelle was still beside me, curled against my chest, her hand resting light as air over my heart. For a few rare minutes, I let myself believe this was all there was—her warmth, her quiet breathing, the weight of her body fitting so perfectly against mine.

Then the phone on my nightstand buzzed. Once. Twice. A third time. Persistent.

I slid out from under her carefully, but she stirred anyway, eyes blinking open, voice husky from sleep.
"Ezra?"

I silenced the phone, glanced at the screen. My jaw tightened.

Board Alert – Emergency Session. Called by Malcolm Price. Noon.

A single line beneath it: *New information regarding the CEO's conduct.*

Of course.

I sat on the edge of the bed, shoulders tight. Noelle pushed herself up, the sheet slipping from her shoulder, her hair a dark tangle around her face. "What is it?"

I turned the phone toward her. She read it quickly, and I saw the way her breath caught. "Malcolm," she whispered, bitterness sharp in her tone.

I nodded once, slipping into the practiced calm I'd learned long ago. "He's trying to use *us*. He thinks dragging you into this will shake me. He doesn't realize I've been ready."

Her brow furrowed. "Ready how?"

I stood, reached for my shirt, buttoned it with care before picking up the phone again. I dialed, and when Marshall

answered, my voice was clipped steel.
"Everything we talked about—it's time. Have the files, the presentation, all of it ready before noon. No gaps, no surprises. I want it airtight."

I paused. "Good. Let Malcolm think he's staging the ambush. We'll be waiting with the floodlights."

I ended the call, turned back to her. She was watching me, equal parts wary and proud.

"You knew this was coming," she said softly.

"I did," I admitted. "Malcolm's never played fair. And I won't let him blindside us. Not you, not me."

She wrapped the sheet tighter around herself, eyes holding mine. "If he's bringing me up in that room, Ezra, I want to be there. I need to stand for myself."

I crossed back to her, lowered myself until we were eye level. My hand slid along her jaw, my thumb brushing her cheekbone. "Then we go together. Not because I need you there, but because I respect that you need to be there."

Her eyes softened, glimmering with something fierce. "Together," she repeated.

I kissed her forehead, lingering there a beat. And as the morning settled heavy around us, I knew one thing with certainty: Malcolm thought he'd called the board to bury me.

But by noon, the ground would shift—and it wouldn't be under my feet.

***

The car rolled to a stop in front of Sinclair Holdings, its mirrored façade catching the morning sun like a weapon. Beside me, Noelle smoothed her skirt with hands that only barely trembled. To anyone else, she looked composed. But I knew her now—the slight pinch between her brows, the way she exhaled through her nose like she was counting her breath. Nerves.

I reached for her hand, threading my fingers through hers, squeezing once. She glanced at me, eyes wide but steady.

"You don't have to do this," I murmured. "One word, and I'll send you home."

Her chin lifted, stubborn even as her pulse fluttered against my thumb. "If they're dragging me into this room, then I'll walk into it myself. I'd rather stand in the fire of the truth than let them write lies about me."

Pride and fear tangled in my chest. She wasn't just brave—she was relentless. And for the first time, I realized how much stronger we were standing side by side.

We stepped out together. The lobby swallowed us whole— marble floors gleaming, the hush of money and power humming like static in the air. The security guard's eyes flicked between us, widening before he quickly dropped them, pretending not to notice. Whispers trailed behind as we crossed the expanse, our joined hands saying everything we hadn't yet announced to the world.

The boardroom doors loomed ahead, heavy walnut, carved with the Sinclair crest. My grip tightened around hers once more. "Last chance," I said quietly, giving her one more out.

Her eyes found mine, unwavering. "I told you already. Together."

I nodded once, then pushed the doors open.

And froze.

It wasn't just the directors inside. Leaning back in one of the leather chairs like he owned it—smile sharp, eyes too knowing—was a face I hadn't expected to see here at all.

Noelle's hand went rigid in mine.

It was her brother, Cal.

***

The air inside the boardroom felt heavier than usual, thick with anticipation. Directors murmured among themselves, pens scratching across paper as though they were already writing my obituary.

But it wasn't the directors who froze me mid-step.

It was him.

Cal.

The night before, he'd worn jeans, a soft shirt, unbridled laughter at a family table. Warm. Familiar. Beloved.

Here, he was someone else entirely. A tailored suit cut to precision. Tie knotted with care. Watch gleaming under the recessed lights. He sat at the table like it belonged to him, posture sharp, every detail curated. The warmth was gone. What remained was power, cold and undeniable.

My gut clenched. Pieces began to shift into place—the charm, the ease, the shadows Noelle never wanted to discuss.

Before I could process it fully, the doors burst open.

Malcolm.

He strode in with a grin stretched too wide, eyes scanning the room until they landed on us. His gaze swept over Noelle, then snagged on her brother, and his smile split wider still.

"Well, well," he drawled, voice carrying across the walnut and glass. "This is even better than I hoped."

Conversations stuttered to a halt. Chairs creaked. Every head turned.

Malcolm spread his hands, pacing to the center like a man about to deliver the performance of his life. "Ladies and gentlemen, I asked for this meeting because I thought Ezra Sinclair's… choices deserved a little daylight. I planned to talk about his new indulgence, Ms. Collins. Her lack of discretion. Her questionable professionalism." He gestured lazily in Noelle's direction, venom wrapped in civility. "But I see we've been given a bonus."

He turned, grin flashing toward her brother. "What's he doing here? No, don't answer—I think I already know."

The silence that followed was brutal. Heavy. Expectant.

My pulse thundered in my ears as Malcolm's gaze cut back to me, glee lighting his face. "Let's talk credibility, Ezra. Yours. Hers. And definitely his."

The room went still. Directors leaned forward. Pens stopped moving. Noelle's hand trembled in mine, her brother's eyes sharp as glass, unreadable.

And in that silence, I knew—we were standing on the edge of a blade.

***

Malcolm

The silence was delicious. Thick, uneasy.

I let it stretch, savoring the tension. Then I turned to the head of the table, to Ezra's father, to Evelyn seated just behind him. "I came here tonight because I thought this board had a right to know exactly who our CEO is surrounding himself with."

Ezra's jaw ticked, but he stayed silent. Cowardly restraint masquerading as control.

I shifted my gaze to Noelle. She was composed on the surface, but I caught the flicker — the way her shoulders tightened, her grip firm on her clutch. She knew.

"Well, let's start with Ms. Collins," I went on, pulling the folder from under my arm and sliding the first page onto the table. "Houston's favorite matchmaker. Self-made, *independent*, sharp enough to convince this city she built her empire from grit alone."

Murmurs circled the table. I waited for them to die before dropping the next page, crisp and damning.

"Except she didn't."

I let that hang, then tipped the page with a single finger. "Seed money came from her brother. A brother she's never mentioned in any interview, any profile, any client dinner. Why? Because he's not the kind of man you parade around."

Gasps rippled. I could feel the shift, the collective inhale.

"He's well known in certain circles," I continued smoothly. "Black market art. Transactions that never see daylight. Galleries scrubbed clean but dirt beneath the polish. The kind of man whose reputation, if tied to this family, would corrode everything we've built. Everything Ezra claims to safeguard."

I glanced around the table, met each director's eyes in turn, and watched doubt sharpen into calculation. Exactly what I wanted.

Finally, I leaned back, smiling like I'd already won. "So tell me, gentlemen and ladies— is this the CEO we want Sinclair Holdings to keep?"

The room went still.

Ezra's face was granite, but his hand clenched tight against the table's edge. Noelle's brother? Still. Too still. His silence louder than any defense.

And Noelle — her composure cracked, just barely, but enough. Enough for everyone to see.

Perfect.

CHAPTER 37

The Spiral and the Fall

Noelle

My stomach dropped so hard it felt like the floor had vanished beneath me.

The words ricocheted around the boardroom — *seed money, black market art, fraud.* Malcolm's voice carried them like knives, polished, sharpened, designed to land where they would cut deepest.

And they did.

Every whisper I'd spent years outrunning, every secret I'd buried under late nights and careful choices, dragged into the light in front of the only people powerful enough to shatter me completely.

My throat tightened until breathing felt impossible. I sat straighter, forced my expression to stay still, to mimic the kind of composure I'd worn into rooms my whole life. But inside? I was unraveling thread by thread.

This is it. This is how it ends. Everything I built reduced to a story that's not even about me or my abilities..

I could feel the heat creeping up my chest, the pulse hammering at my temple. My parents' faces flickered in my mind—my mother's voice telling me to walk in like I belonged, my father's pride when I signed my first client. What would they see now, if they could see me? A fraud dressed in silk.

Don't cry. Don't move. Don't give them the satisfaction.

And then—

A sound. Low, unexpected.

Cal laughed.

It wasn't loud. It wasn't unhinged. Just a quiet, amused chuckle that rolled out of him like the whole thing was a parlor trick, not a blade to my throat.

I whipped my head toward him, panic spiking sharper. *What are you doing?* My eyes begged the question I couldn't say aloud.

But he just leaned back in his chair, relaxed, almost indulgent, like Malcolm's accusations were nothing more than smoke he could wave away when the time suited him.

Around the table, the silence deepened. Directors shifted uncomfortably, caught between scandal and curiosity. Ezra's hand slid against mine under the table, steady, grounding, but even his touch couldn't quiet the storm inside me.

Because all I could think was: *Maybe Malcolm was right. Maybe I'd been fooling myself this whole time. Maybe this was the moment the life I'd built finally collapsed, and all that would be left was the shadow of the brother I could never escape.*

My brother rose slowly, unhurried, the kind of deliberate movement that made people lean in before he'd even spoken. His suit caught the light, his presence filling the room as if he owned the air itself.

"Tell me, Malcolm," he began, voice smooth, cutting through the tension like a blade through silk. "What proof do you have of such ridiculous claims?"

Malcolm's smile tightened. "I have a source."

My brother tilted his head, as though considering a child's answer. "A source. Convenient." He stepped closer to the table, hands clasped lightly behind his back. "Then let's not waste the board's time with stories. Call your source. Right now. Put him on speaker so we can all hear the truth."

Malcolm's eyes flicked, quick as a tell. "I don't answer to you."

For a moment, the room stilled. And then—

Ezra's father leaned forward, his voice carrying the full weight of his authority. "Call him."

It wasn't a suggestion. It was command.

Smug, almost gloating, Malcolm slipped his phone from his pocket. "Gladly." He scrolled, tapped, set it to speaker, and placed it on the table like he was about to win the final hand.

The line rang once. Twice.

Then the voice. Flat. Mechanical. Final.

This number has been disconnected.

The words echoed, devastating in the silence that followed.

Something fractured. Not just in the air, but in Malcolm. The smug curve of his mouth faltered for the first time, his fingers twitching against the phone before he snatched it back as if hiding the evidence of his own failure.

Around the table, the directors shifted. A few exchanged looks. A murmur rose, the tide turning, suspicion seeping not toward my brother—but toward Malcolm.

And all I could think, pulse hammering in my ears, was that this was only the beginning.

.***

My brother smirked, then adjusted his cuff, calm as if Malcolm's stumble had only confirmed what he already suspected. I knew him enough to know no one would be hearing from that person ever again.

"That's interesting," he said lightly, almost conversational. "So you've accused me of crimes. With no proof. That, Mr. Sinclair, is defamation."

The word landed like a strike. The board shifted, uneasy.

Malcolm's mask cracked, his voice pitching sharper. "What—what did you do?!"

My brother tilted his head, smile cool. "More false accusations. No accountability. Just deflection. Predictable."

The silence that followed felt like a fuse burning low. And then Ezra stepped forward.

"Malcolm." His voice carried steady, cutting clean through the room. He lifted a hand toward the corner, and the screen flickered to life — the blue glow giving way to the first slide of a deck already waiting. "If we're going to talk about credibility, let's deal in facts. And this time, I've brought proof."

Malcolm froze, the color draining from his face.

Ezra's tone stayed calm, almost surgical. "You've implied I'm distracted. That I can't lead. But what this board deserves to ask is why *you* believe you're fit to hold this chair."

Malcolm seized his script like a lifeline. "Because I'm married. Because Vivienne and I represent stability. Partnership. That's what this company needs—"

Ezra clicked the remote.

A photo filled the screen — grainy but damning. Malcolm in a hotel lobby, his hand low on a woman's back, her face tipped toward his.

Gasps swept the table.

"Tell me, Malcolm," Ezra said smoothly, "is this your wife?"

Malcolm lurched halfway out of his chair. "That—that isn't what it looks like—"

Click. Another photo. Another woman. A timestamp stamped clear as day.

The air thickened. The directors leaned in, the shift in the room unmistakable.

Ezra didn't raise his voice. He didn't need to. "Or would you prefer we move on to numbers?" He clicked again. The slide changed to rows of figures — accounts, transfers, every digit damning. "I decided to look into the work you've been putting in. What I found was shocking to say the least. Money. Six million dollars. Moved under your hand. Stolen."

The silence that followed was suffocating.

Malcolm's hands shook against the table. His mouth opened, but nothing came. His confidence, his smirk, the certainty he'd carried into the room — gone.

Beside me, Ezra's hand closed over mine, firm, grounding. I realized I was trembling too, though not from fear.

Because Ezra hadn't just shielded me. He'd turned the boardroom into a courtroom, and the verdict had been written in real time.

Malcolm Price hadn't just lost the fight.

He'd been exposed.

CHAPTER 38

The Reckoning

Ezra

I'd delivered the blow, but I couldn't take all the credit. The file containing the affair pictures, and a tip to check the accounts hadn't come from me. It had come from Noelle's brother—slid across the table after Sunday dinner with the kind of calm that told me he'd already measured me and decided I was worth trusting.

And that unsettled me almost as much as it steadied me.

Because that kind of information—bank records, photos, timestamps—doesn't just fall into anyone's lap. It takes reach. Leverage. Power.

I had expected a wary older brother, ready to test my intentions. What I hadn't expected was a man who could hand me the ammunition to dismantle Malcolm Price in front of an entire board.

I found myself staring, impressed despite everything. The charm he'd worn at Sunday dinner was still there, but sharpened now, wielded like a weapon. Calculated. Dangerous. And yet—he was on our side. On hers.

The scrape of a chair broke the silence. I started to rise, ready to speak, but Vivienne moved faster. She crossed the room in heels that cracked like gunfire against the marble and stopped in front of Malcolm.

Her hand flew.

The sound rang louder than any gavel.

Malcolm's head snapped to the side, his cheek already flaming red. He didn't even have time to react before Vivienne's voice cut through the stunned quiet.

"I want a divorce."

Her words trembled but her spine didn't. She looked at him like he was a stranger, like the years they'd spent together were ash in her mouth. Then her chin lifted, eyes glassy, and she turned—walking out without another word, tears streaking against the steel of her expression.

The door shut behind her, and the room exhaled as if no one had remembered how to breathe until now.

Noelle's brother let the silence stretch, then gestured lightly toward the screen. His tone was calm, almost bored.

"As you can see, Mr. Malcolm here has been busy. What I'd like to know is this—are you going to allow an employee of this company to speak defamatory comments about me and my sister without consequence?"

All eyes swung to the head of the table.

My father's face was thunder. His hand clenched against the wood so tightly the veins stood out stark. "Enough." His voice was clipped steel. "Malcolm, you are finished here."

Malcolm lurched forward. "Wait—"

"Save it." My father's tone left no room. "You've embarrassed this family, this company, and yourself. Security will escort you out. Effective immediately."

The weight of the words landed like a gavel, final and merciless. Chairs shifted, whispers rippled, but no one challenged him.

Malcolm's face twisted—rage, fear, disbelief—but it didn't matter. His power was gone, stripped clean in front of everyone.

I looked at Noelle. She was pale, hands tight in her lap, but her brother's arm rested easily on the chair beside her, steadying her without even touching.

And for the first time, I saw it clearly: the Collins siblings weren't bystanders They were a force.

***

My father's decree still hung in the air, heavy as stone, when security moved toward Malcolm. He sputtered, tried to gather himself, but the fight was already gone from him. The directors avoided his eyes, papers shuffled, a few throats cleared — everyone eager to move on, to distance themselves from the stench of a man just dismantled.

I should have felt nothing but relief. Instead, I scanned the table, noting every reaction.

And then my gaze landed on her.

My mother.

Evelyn Sinclair — the woman who could silence a room with a raised brow, who had praised Alexandra Martin as if she were hand-selected by God himself.

She wasn't angry. Not in the way I expected.

She was watching Noelle's brother.

Not with disdain. Not even with suspicion. With something that looked uncomfortably close to interest…maybe even admiration. Her lips pursed, her head tilted just slightly — as if she was measuring the man, recalibrating a chessboard in real time.

The realization unsettled me more than Malcolm's implosion. My mother didn't get intrigued. She got certain. And if she was reconsidering, that meant the ground beneath us was already shifting.

I tightened my jaw, sliding my gaze toward Noelle. She sat stiff, her eyes fixed on the table, but her brother leaned back like a man who had done exactly what he came to do.

For the first time in my life, Evelyn Sinclair and I were looking at the same person — and both acknowledging, silently, that he was someone worth watching.

And that… that could change everything.

＊＊

The room was still vibrating with the aftershock when Cal pushed back his chair. The scrape was deliberate, commanding. He rose with the kind of poise that made every director sit straighter, as though instinctively bracing against the force of him.

"Well," he said, voice smooth, unhurried. "It looks like my part here is done." His gaze swept the table, lingering just long enough on each face to make them feel seen—and implicated. Then he smiled, warm as if this were nothing more than a dinner party. "Thank you, Harrington. And you, Mrs. Patel. And of course, Mr. Singh. For the invitation."

The names landed like blows. Connections revealed. Alliances confirmed.

Not just a man dragged in by scandal. A man who had walked in with more friends in this room than Malcolm ever realized.

He buttoned his jacket, collected his phone, and inclined his head toward my father with the faintest curve of amusement. Then, like a hurricane that had swept through, exposed rot, and stripped the walls bare, he was gone.

The silence he left behind was deafening.

I rose, my voice steady. "Before we adjourn, I'd like to make something clear." My eyes cut to Malcolm's empty chair, then back to the board. "Meridian is complete. Ahead of schedule. Under budget. The deliverables have been met, audited, and signed off. The condition you set for my two month extension has been satisfied."

A stir moved through the room. Harrington looked over his glasses, blinking. Another director shuffled his papers, confirming what I'd just said.

My father's gaze stayed locked on me. Cold. Testing. Finally, he gave one sharp nod. "Then the extension stands."

I didn't let myself breathe, not yet. Not until I saw their expressions shift, the tide turning again—this time not with doubt, but with something closer to respect.

"Good," I said simply. "Then we're finished here."

I gathered my notes with precise movements, my jaw tight against the storm still inside me. Because while the boardroom was contained, the cost wasn't.

Vivienne's face flashed in my mind—her tears, her voice breaking as she told Malcolm she wanted out.

And I knew where I needed to be.

The boardroom emptied like a storm tide retreating—papers shuffled, voices low, chairs scraping. But Vivienne had been the first wave gone, her heels sharp against the marble as she fled. I should've followed immediately, but my father's decree, my mother's unreadable expression, the mess Malcolm left behind—they'd all pulled at me until I finally forced myself out.

I found her by the elevators. Not pacing, not crying, just standing there with her arms locked around herself, staring at her reflection in the chrome doors. The slap she'd given Malcolm still echoed in my head—sharp, decisive—but now, stripped of that adrenaline, she looked smaller. Tired.

"Viv," I said softly.

She turned, eyes catching mine. Not cold. Not distant. Just raw.

"I should've seen it," she said, her voice low, uneven. "I should've known what he was doing. I've lived in this family long enough to recognize rot."

"You did see it," I reminded her. "You warned me. You gave me the chance to brace for him before he went after me."

Her mouth twisted, the weight of it dragging at her. "I warned you because I didn't want to see him take you down. But I never thought it would be me he gutted first." She shook her head, blinking hard, refusing tears. "Ten years married, Ezra. Ten years. And I didn't know him at all."

I stepped closer, keeping my voice steady. "That's not your failure, Vivienne. That's his."

She searched my face, like she was testing whether I really believed it, then gave a shaky laugh. "You sound so sure of yourself all of a sudden."

"Not sure of myself," I said. "Sure of you. You didn't let him walk out with lies intact. You ended it, in front of everyone. That took more than strength. That took guts."

Her eyes glistened, but the tears stayed put. "When was the last time we talked like this? No strategies or business."

I almost smiled. "When we were kids, sneaking cookies off the silver trays before galas."

That tugged something real out of her—a small smile, fragile but alive. "You always blamed me when we got caught."

"And you always forgave me," I said.

The silence that followed wasn't brittle anymore. It carried weight, but it felt like something worth holding, even if we didn't quite know how.

When the elevator chimed, she pressed the button, then paused before stepping in. She looked back at me, chin high, eyes soft.
"Thank you," she said.

"You're welcome," I told her, meeting her gaze.

Then she stepped inside, the doors closing on her perfume and that faint, unpolished smile. For the first time in years, she didn't feel like my critic or my rival. She felt like my sister again.

***

Noelle

The corridors were nearly empty by the time I slipped free of the boardroom's echo. My pulse hadn't caught up yet—still thundering in my ears like the meeting hadn't ended, like Malcolm's accusations and my brother's thunderous rebuttal were still vibrating off the walls.

I found him outside, near the porte-cochère, where the Sinclair driver pool idled. He looked like he'd just stepped off a magazine page: suit pressed, tie loose, posture at ease as if he'd been waiting for me. No hint of the storm he'd just unleashed inside.

"How did you do it?" The question came out before I could stop it, sharper than I meant.

He smiled, faint but knowing, and reached out to squeeze my shoulder. "I told you once, didn't I? I always keep my word."

"That's not an answer." My voice broke on the edges. "You.."

He pulled me into a hug before I could press further. Warm. Familiar. The kind of embrace that made me want to forget the shadows he carried. His chin rested lightly against my hair as he murmured, "You don't need every answer, Elle. You just need to know I've got you."

For a moment, I let myself sink into it—into the feeling of knowing I can always rely on my brother. His heartbeat was steady, his grip protective, and I felt safe.

When he pulled back, his smile had returned, gentle and unreadable all at once. "I'll be in touch," he said, and with that he turned toward a waiting car.

I stood there watching the taillights disappear, my throat tight. I should've known better than to underestimate him. He'd always had a way of making storms vanish—or at least look like they had.

And yet, instead of fear, what I felt most was relief.

Relief that he was my brother.

Relief that—he always had my back.

CHAPTER 39

Always

Noelle

The flight was short, but the silence between us felt longer. Ezra kept my hand in his the entire drive from the airport, his thumb tracing slow, thoughtful lines against my skin. Neither of us spoke. It wasn't an uncomfortable quiet—it was the kind that comes when words would only make too much noise.

When the car turned off the coastal road, I lowered the window and breathed in the sea. Salt, pine, and sunlight wove through the air—cleaner, freer than the heat and hum of Houston. The villa appeared ahead, pale stone against the water, half-wrapped in vines and sunlight, like it had been waiting for us to arrive.

"Why here?" I asked as we slowed up the drive.

Ezra looked toward the horizon, his profile calm, unguarded. "Because it's far enough that the world can't reach us," he said. "And close enough that we can find our way back if we need to."

The answer wasn't poetic. It was him—simple, direct, deliberate. And it felt right.

Inside, the villa opened into sunlight and ocean breeze. Curtains lifted with the wind, carrying the scent of salt and something citrusy from the trees outside. A bottle of wine waited on the table beside two crystal glasses. Ezra dropped our bags and stretched, rolling the tension from his shoulders.

"Come here," he said softly, and I did—because I always did.

By midafternoon, the villa had gone soft and golden, the air thick with salt and sunlight. The sound of waves carried up from below, slow and rhythmic, as if the sea itself had exhaled.

Two masseuses arrived with warm oils and soft linen sheets, moving quietly across the terrace. They set up side by side, their carts clinking faintly, the faint scent of jasmine and citrus drifting through the open doors.

I lay face down first, cheek turned toward the breeze, while practiced hands found every knot along my shoulders.

The tension I'd been carrying—weeks of small fractures and unspoken things—started to ease beneath her touch. My body felt heavier, but in the good way. Anchored.

Across from me, Ezra's voice floated through the warmth. Low, even, and unhurried. He was talking to his masseuse about the villa, the view, the kind of meaningless things people only say when they've finally run out of noise. His tone had that particular calm I only ever heard when he was far from everything that demanded him.

When I turned my head, I caught him in profile—bare chest, sun on his skin, lashes half-lowered, his mouth curved in quiet contentment. His hands hung loose at his sides, his whole body slack with ease.

I don't think I'd ever seen him look so human. So unarmored.

It stirred something low in me—not lust exactly, though that was there too—but a kind of ache. A tenderness for the man he was when the world stopped asking things of him.

He must've felt me looking, because without opening his eyes, he said, "You know, it's hard to relax when the most beautiful woman I've ever seen keeps staring at me."

My masseuse laughed softly under her breath. I smiled into the sheet. "Maybe she's just admiring the scenery."

Ezra finally cracked an eye open, and that familiar glint returned. "Then I guess I owe the view some competition."

Later, we swam.

The water was warm, still kissed by the last of the afternoon sun. From the edge of the infinity pool, the sea stretched out below us—blue folding into deeper blue.

I floated on my back, eyes half closed, the sun tracing its way across my skin. Ezra's strokes cut through the water beside me, slow and deliberate, sending gentle ripples that rocked me back and forth.

Every now and then, he'd dive beneath the surface and brush his fingers along my ankle as he passed, the smallest touch—enough to make me laugh each time.

When I lifted my head, he was leaning against the far ledge, elbows braced, water beading on his shoulders. His hair was slicked back, his eyes soft.

"Now you're the one staring," I said, smiling.

He didn't deny it. "It's hard not to."

I swam closer until the water lapped against his chest. "You've seen me a hundred times."

He caught my wrist beneath the surface, thumb dragging slow circles against my skin. "And every time I do, I wonder how I got this lucky."

My throat tightened—not from surprise, but because he said it like it was the most ordinary truth in the world.

"Ezra—"

He shook his head, voice barely above a whisper. "Don't downplay it. You have this way of making everything around you look… worth stopping for."

I didn't know what to say to that, so I didn't. I just let him pull me in until our bodies aligned, water slick and warm between us.

He kissed me then—slow, deep, without hurry. The world narrowed to sunlight, salt, and breath. His hand slid up the back of my neck, anchoring me there, and for a moment it felt like we were suspended somewhere outside of time—two people who'd already lived a hundred versions of love, finding one more.

When he finally drew back, his forehead rested against mine.

"Let's stay right here," he murmured. "Just like this."

And for once, I didn't think about what came next.

The waves kept their rhythm below, the light spilled gold across the water, and everything else could wait.

By evening, the air turned soft and amber. We wandered down to the small artist's square near the cliff, stopping when an older man waved us over. His easel leaned toward the light, a half-finished portrait in strokes of gold and brown.

"You two—sit," he insisted, gesturing to a bench. "You look like a story worth keeping."

I laughed, embarrassed. Ezra just shrugged and settled beside me.

The artist studied us for a long moment before sketching. "Married?" he asked, pencil moving fast.

"Not yet," Ezra answered easily.

"Ah," the man said, smiling. "Then this one—" he nodded toward me "—will make it last."

I didn't look at Ezra, but I felt the way his hand found mine and stayed there.

Dinner came late, slow and lingering.

The terrace was washed in gold from the candles scattered across the table, their flames bending with the breeze. The sea below murmured against the rocks, a steady sound that filled the spaces between our words.

We ate slowly—fresh fish drizzled with lemon, roasted vegetables slick with olive oil, bread still warm from the oven. The kind of meal meant to be shared without hurry. Ezra poured the wine, deep red catching the firelight, and with every glass, the tension in his shoulders eased.

He didn't say much, but then again, he didn't need to. His eyes did most of the talking—quiet glances that lingered a second too long, soft smiles that said more than conversation could. I could feel the day peeling away from both of us, leaving something unguarded behind.

When the plates were cleared, music drifted from a nearby villa—something slow and unassuming, a melody wrapped in nostalgia.

Ezra stood and held out a hand, the candlelight carving his features into shadow and gold. "Dance with me," he said.

I smiled, shaking my head. "There's no room."

"There's enough." His voice was calm, certain. "There's always enough."

I slid my hand into his, and he pulled me close.

His palm found the small of my back, fingers spreading in slow, steady pressure. My other hand rested against his chest, feeling the slow, deliberate beat beneath. The rhythm was uneven, our steps unpracticed, but neither of us cared.

We moved anyway—barefoot on the cool tile, tipsy from the wine and the weightlessness of being untethered. The night air wrapped around us, warm with the scent of salt and citrus, candle smoke curling lazily in the air.

Ezra's chin brushed the top of my head. "You smell like the ocean," he murmured, voice rough.

"And you smell like trouble," I said, smiling against his shirt.

His laugh was low, genuine—the kind that came from somewhere deep. "That's accurate."

We swayed in silence for a while. My cheek against his shoulder. His fingers drawing idle shapes against the curve of my spine. The song changed, but we didn't.

"This," I whispered finally, the words more breath than sound, "feels unfair."

He glanced down at me, a faint smile curving the corner of his mouth. "Why?"

"Because it's too perfect not to end."

Ezra's gaze lingered on me for a long moment, something unspoken moving behind it—something like promise, something like fear. Then he dipped his head, his mouth brushing mine, soft at first, then deeper.

It wasn't urgent. It wasn't even about wanting. It was about *knowing*.

The kiss stretched slow, unhurried, until the world around us blurred—the music, the sea, even the candlelight fading to nothing but warmth and skin and breath.

When we finally broke apart, the night hummed with silence, heavy and alive. He pressed his forehead to mine, his thumb grazing my jaw.

"You think too much," he said quietly.

"Someone has to."

"Not tonight."

The words came out almost a command, but softened by the way he looked at me—like he'd already decided that, for once, the world could wait.

So I didn't argue. I just let him pull me closer until my body fit against his like memory.

The music drifted on, and we kept moving long after the song ended, our rhythm slow and imperfect, our steps small enough to stay inside the circle of candlelight.

And for a while—maybe for the rest of the night—it was enough.

Morning came slow and bright. I woke to Ezra's arm heavy across my waist, his breath steady against my neck. The air was still warm from the night before, carrying the faint scent of salt and wine.

When I turned, he was already awake, watching me. His voice was rough with sleep. "You're incredible, you know that?"

"Mm," I murmured, smiling. "You might be too."

He brushed his thumb along my jaw, the gesture familiar but still enough to undo me. "Stay right here," he said.

And I might've.

If not for—

A knock at the villa door.

Firm. Measured. Too early for housekeeping.

Ezra's hand went still against me. Another knock followed, louder this time.

We froze, caught between breath and the echo of what we'd built here.

Whoever was outside, they didn't belong to this quiet.

And just like that—the world had found us again.

If you enjoyed this book, follow along for new releases, sneak peeks and more at Tamickaleonard.com and on Tiktok and Facebook @authortfleonard.